THE
PEACE
MACHINE

THE PEACE MACHINE

OZGUR MUMCU

Translated by
MARK DAVID WYERS

PUSHKIN PRESS

Pushkin Press
71–75 Shelton Street
London WC2H 9JQ

Original text © Özgür Mumcu / Kalem Agency 2016
English translation © Mark David Wyers 2018

The Peace Machine was first published as
Barış makinesi in Istanbul, 2016

First published by Pushkin Press in 2018

1 3 5 7 9 8 6 4 2

ISBN 13: 978 1 78227 394 3

Designed and typeset by Tetragon, London
Printed in Great Britain by the CPI Group, UK

www.pushkinpress.com

CONTENTS

1   The Tangles of a Tongue-Twister   7

2   A Halal Duel   17

3   Checkmate!   35

4   The Winged Bats are Right   45

5   The Hubris of Might   63

6   Wild Cherries   75

7   The Young Lieutenant   95

8   A Fool's Aid   105

9   The Doomed Palace   115

10 The Death of a Corpse   127

11 The Circus Dervish   153

12 The Mummified Lion   177

13 Timelessness   187

14 A Rather Trying Matter   191

15 The Peace Machine   213

I

The Tangles of a Tongue-Twister

"THE COLD CUT ME to the quick / There was an apple that I picked / Plucked from a tree that was taller than me / 'But you're a pygmy' they quipped / 'No bigger than a pippysqueak pip.'"

Celal had no choice but to run. The only way he could run, however, was by saying tongue-twisters. If he stumbled over the words of a tongue-twister, he'd trip and topple to the ground. And if he couldn't get started with one, he'd go as limp as a puppet whose strings had been cut.

"Sister, sister, cooking rice in a pot / A rat fell in, plop, plop, plop…"

In fact he was still growing, he didn't have a sister, and it had been three months since he'd had a bowl of rice. There was a rat in the cellar where he'd been locked up the night before, and he smacked his lips at the thought of devouring it. Still, the rat was anything but pygmy-sized and Celal knew it was bent on taking a bite out of his ear. They tussled and scuffled throughout the night so that Celal didn't get a wink of sleep.

Nor did he pee. By morning his bladder was on the verge of bursting, but he wasn't just trying to be civil. No, he knew how to take on grown men in a fight and he had a plan.

"If you can't win with your fists, use your wits. A trick is only a trick if you're already strong enough to win in a brawl." Süleyman had said that. And he was right. Of course he was right. That's why he had the best pocket knife around. If he hadn't deserved it, the big boys would've taken it away.

The owner of the shop above the cellar was a large man, so big that not even Süleyman could've taken him on. But that was beside the point because Süleyman couldn't have come anyway. Two weeks earlier, he'd fallen over face first after botching a tongue-twister while running, and the blade of his pocket knife had jabbed into his crotch. Blood had squirted from the wound like water from a fountain, spattering Celal's face. Celal had been so scared that he'd dashed off without even thinking of taking the knife.

Celal had been planning to steal three eggs and a quarter loaf of bread that he'd tucked under his shirt. The owner usually didn't notice such things, so it was a carpet trader with a pock-marked face who had caught Celal and grabbed him by the ear. Celal hadn't seen it coming.

Süleyman had once said, "In our holy Hadiths the Prophet says that the poor will get into heaven five hundred years before the rich." But that didn't do Celal any good. The shop owner had grabbed his other ear and slapped him across the face so hard that his nose bled till dawn.

The shop owner unlocked the cellar door just before the morning call to prayer. Celal was standing at the ready, his ragged underpants down around his ankles. He fired a stream of urine into the shop owner's face with such force that the man was stunned for a moment. Celal yanked up his underpants, dashed between the man's legs and ran up the stairs to the shop entrance. Luckily the door wasn't locked, which meant that the owner had gone out to do his ablutions before going down to the cellar. *All the better*, Celal thought. *You'll have to do them again before you can pray!*

"...Rat, rat, this is what you get / We'll throw you from the minaret / There's a bird up there with silvery wings / And uncle's pockets are full of shiny things."

Celal snatched a chicken from the yard as he ran out. He hadn't planned on killing it right away, but it kept clucking under his arm, making him forget the words to the tongue-twister, so in order to say the tongue-twister he had to break the chicken's neck. It was as simple as that.

So be it, he thought. *The chicken will get into heaven all the sooner!*

The fate of a chicken can be fraught with surprises. First you go from being a hatchling to a chick and learn about the difference between pebbles and corn kernels, and then before you know it you find yourself stuffed under the arm of a bloody-nosed boy with a shaved head, as he bolts down a deserted road which is a three-week journey from the town of Shkodra, panting tongue-twisters all the while.

And there you are, your head flopping back and forth on your broken neck.

But since history is never written by the losers, the chicken's tale ends there. Celal cooked it up and gobbled up half of it. The rest he traded for a ragged felt blanket, and that was the last he thought of the bird. The blanket, however, wouldn't be forgotten so easily. Winter had swept in with unusual ferocity that year.

That winter, and for many winters to follow, Celal had to say tongue-twisters to save his hide.

"Work till you're dead / For a simple piece of bread / But the cat stole my lunch / Crunch, crunch, crunch."

One time the head of the beggars' guild tried to break Celal's arm, and Celal headbutted him so hard that the bone of the poor Pomak's nose was shoved into his brain. Afterwards, Celal ran not one but two provinces away.

"My stomach is rumbling / Well, stop your grumbling / And run to the mill / But the door is locked / And the stork's bill is pocked."

Those were the words he said as he ran off at midday from a bathhouse furnace where he'd found work with six other boys. Celal had put up with the bullying from Long-Legged Cafer, the head furnace keeper, but when he tried to send Celal to work as a bath attendant on account of his youth and comely features, he'd emptied a shovelful of burning coals over the furnace keeper's head and run away.

"Down by the bay / Baby goats and billy goats browse day by day / I said, Why do the baby goats and billy goats browse by the bay? / They said, Baby goats and billy goats browse and play / Baa-bay bay-baa it's always been that way."

The older he got the faster Celal could run, and the faster he could run the longer tongue-twisters he could say. He took up stealing goats in the hills of Edirne, but over time he grew weary of being driven off by angry shepherds. He sold the last goats he'd stolen in a small village and bought two suckling lambs. With the leftover money he bought himself some new clothes, and in return for the lambs a butcher promised him a job at a slaughterhouse in Istanbul.

The sun was rising as a French mail ship sailed past Saray-burnu. As the ship approached the Karaköy quay, the passengers on deck took in the stillness of Istanbul. A curtain of silence hung over the city, and the only sound was the squawking of a gull.

As the morning call to prayer drifted from minaret to minaret, the metropolis was still groggy but slowly stirring itself awake. It was the middle of spring. Judas trees bloomed along the shores of the Bosphorus as if by divine command, casting a purplish-pink glow on the strait's waters. Dawn gave way to day, lighting up the city's seaward windows one by one with a reddish glimmer until the hills along the Bosphorus seemed to erupt in flames.

The ship cleft the calm sea like a blade, leaving behind a wound that closed with splashes of foam. The packs of dogs that haunted the shores of Karaköy joined the emerging chorus of seagulls with their yips and barks. Everything was just as it should be on a glorious spring day in the year 1880.

The passengers could now see people moving about on shore. Some were heading towards mosques and others were opening their shops, and beggars sleeping on the streets began to waken. One of the more astute observers on deck saw that there was a bull pacing back and forth at the end of the quay. The bull paused, looked at the approaching ship and the shores of Üsküdar across the strait, and then it lowed mournfully. Scratching at the quay with its front hoof, the bull slowly turned and looked back. A crowd was approaching, but when the people saw its firm, fierce gaze, they stopped, and with a bellow that echoed through the streets of Karaköy, the bull leapt into the Bosphorus.

After swimming past the ship, the bull paddled calmly towards the Maiden's Tower. Once there it got caught up in the current and disappeared beneath the waves, but moments later its head reappeared. A young gull swooped down and landed on one of the bull's horns, and it swam the rest of the way to Üsküdar. Now that it was on shore the bull tossed its head, sending the gull on its way, and shook the water from its coat before ambling to Mihrimah Mosque, where it entered the courtyard. The sun shining down between the mosque's two minarets blinded the bull for a moment, but soon enough it curled up in a corner and fell asleep.

As the bull lay down, a commotion was rippling through the streets on the opposite shore. People were gathering on the pier, in the courtyards of mosques and in front of shops, and then they suddenly scattered in all directions. A bull appeared on one of the streets, driving a group of people before it. Then there were two bulls, and then three, four, five, and they kept coming until they filled the city's streets in a frenzied swarm of hooves and horns.

They shattered the shop windows and gored whoever crossed their path, regardless of religion, creed or sect. The packs of dogs wandering the streets were trampled under their feet. They gathered in groups and knocked down rickety wood buildings. As they thundered along, an impenetrable cloud of dust enveloped the city. Blinded, hundreds of bulls tumbled into the sea. The captain of the ship, which was now surrounded by bulls floundering in the water, steered for the open sea. Frothing at the mouth, the bulls struck the ship's metal hull with their horns, but eventually their strength gave out and they started drowning, one by one.

Like an invading army, bulls took over every corner of the city, and some of them started goring each other. The clattering of horns joined the cacophony of screams, bellows and ululations as people tried to round up the bulls.

Here's how it had happened: the owner of the slaughter-house where Celal worked was keen on new technologies.

For the upcoming Feast of the Sacrifice he had a telegraph sent to a trader in Tekirdağ, asking for a hundred bulls. But the telegraph operator, who happened to be new on the job, ordered a thousand bulls by mistake. Replying that he would need three months to gather the livestock, the trader sent out word to the four corners of Rumelia. He managed to get the thousand bulls, but in the end there wasn't a sire left in the land. Having sold everything he had, the trader decided to take the herd of bulls to Istanbul himself with the help of some shepherds. When he was unable to pay their wages on arrival, however, the shepherds abandoned the herd, which then went on a rampage through the city.

Why the trader never stopped to ask why anyone would want to buy a thousand bulls would always remain a mystery, because he was the first victim of the stampede. He was trampled to death by fifty-seven bulls in Silivri on the outskirts of Istanbul.

For three days the bulls overran the city, and a regiment had to be brought in from Thessaloniki to bring them under control. By the time it was over, the seven districts of Istanbul were in ruins and seven thousand people had lost their lives, including two government ministers. Among locals the event became known as the "Flight of the Bulls", and it gave rise to the tradition of painting a bull in bright colours and driving it into the sea. Even today, it's not uncommon for people to come across the skeletons of bulls when they dig wells.

One bull, which had an eye dangling from its socket—the result of a tussle with another bull—made its way from Tophane to Boğazkesen and started clambering up the steep road. Celal was hot on its heels, clutching a lasso, hoping to get into the slaughterhouse owner's good graces by bringing him one of the bulls.

According to a certain fortune-teller whose path Celal had crossed some days earlier, his luck was about to change. The poor woman was far from pleasant to behold: her clothes were tattered, she was little more than skin and bones and she walked doubled over. Celal had taken pity on her. He had wrapped up some scraps of offal in greaseproof paper and given them to the woman. Before taking away the spleen, liver and intestines, the fortune-teller spread them on the ground and read Celal's fortune, saying that his future was bright and that fortune would smile upon him.

On the day of the "Flight of the Bulls", Celal's only thought was of rounding up the bull and perhaps getting a few coins for his efforts. As he saw it, it was impossible to know when his luck would turn, if it would turn at all, and he saw no point in putting any faith in the words of a half-baked fortune-teller.

With surprising speed the nearly one-ton bull made its way up to the Grande Rue de Pera, Istanbul's most fashionable street at the time, where it started charging back and forth, unimpeded by the presence of any other bulls. When it charged some horses pulling a tram, they reared up, throwing the driver to the ground and trampling him underfoot. The bull continued up the boulevard towards the Imperial Galatasaray High School, wreaking havoc along the way. Trying to stay out of harm's way, a well-dressed man was huddling against the wall of the high school, but to no avail. The enraged bull approached him, horns lowered. Just as it was about to charge, Celal ran in front of the bull. Staring into its one eye, Celal raised his fist and brought it down on the bull's head with such force that it toppled to the ground in a heap.

The well-dressed man straightened up and took a few unsteady steps towards the bull. In the meantime, Celal was staring at his fist in astonishment. That one act of heroism had shown him how strong he was, despite his youth. The man threw his arms around Celal and took him by the hand, leading him down the street. Celal walked along beside him, his lasso trailing along the ground. After passing through a large garden that was home to two peacocks, they arrived at a mansion. Once inside, the man locked the doors and windows and, with the help of the house servants, pushed a heavy side table up against the front door. He turned to Celal and said, "You saved my life. From now on, I shall raise you as if you were my own son."

And so Celal the streetwise orphan began to live like a prince. At that moment he swore that he would never say a tongue-twister ever again—it was now time for him to start making promises he could never keep.

2

A Halal Duel

I F CELAL HAD STAYED PUT at the bar of the Hotel d'Angleterre, things might not have ended so calamitously. He was properly attired for the place: navy-blue trousers, a matching frock coat, a white shirt and a camel-hair overcoat. Anyone who saw his cravat, tied in a single knot neatly held in place with a gleaming silver pin, would have surmised that this gentleman must be a regular at the Café Concordia or other establishments frequented by the city's elite.

As Celal nursed a glass of cognac, savouring its woody flavours, he fancied that he'd make an impression on the women swishing around in their fine gowns. But one cognac led to another, and ultimately he would spend the evening with women of much more dubious character.

Debonair in his frock coat, Celal turned into Flower Street, which rang with the sound of hurdy-gurdy music. He knew that high-ceilinged ballrooms could not offer what he sought—what he needed could only be found in the dingy cabarets around the district of Galata. He picked one at random and went inside. In a corner, a musician was playing a tune that was particular to Istanbul's Bakla Horani Carnival. A tall young woman with twin braids was singing along, swaying to the music. The cabaret was packed. Celal shouldered his way into the crowd. A mild glass of wine took the edge off the cognac he'd been drinking and he stood there for a while, listening to the music.

Everything should have unfolded rather simply. Someone would catch his eye and then they would head upstairs. But Celal hadn't yet grasped the fact that simple things have to be handled delicately. He approached a woman who was voluptuous, graced with firm curves. Unfortunately for Celal, however, at that very moment another man was walking up to the same woman. If Celal and the man hadn't clashed like bulls, everything would have proceeded without a hitch.

Celal later remembered that he had argued with the man in French, but it didn't dawn on him that he'd given the man his name and address until a letter arrived two days later.

My esteemed Celal Bey,

I am deeply grieved by the fact that we met under such regrettable circumstances the other night. On the condition that you apologize for the altercation that occurred between us, I would like to turn our encounter into an honourable matter rather than one of grievances. My own honour, however, which was tarnished by your untoward aggression, must first receive due compensation. So I have no choice but to await your apology, which shall be delivered by post to the address below. Otherwise,

I will have no choice but to challenge you to a duel, which would be nothing short of unfortunate.

Karachiyano, ambassadorial translator

Dismissing the letter as childish, Celal tossed it aside and asked his servant whether or not his bath had been drawn. Although he had become embroiled in an argument, in the end he'd gone upstairs with the woman he desired. And he didn't go home the following morning, but the following midnight. He was comforted by the thought that a thorough scrub would wash away his weariness and soothe his body, which ached from head to toe.

The bath revived him. After pouring a sixth scoop of warm water over his head, he decided to reply to Karachiyano's letter. While he found the whole business utterly ridiculous, he didn't want to give anyone the chance to think he was a coward.

Celal went up to his room and put on a dressing gown. He pulled a pipe from his pocket, lit it and went into his study. He sat down at his cherry-wood desk, which had been delivered just a week before, and pulled a piece of Willcox paper from a drawer. Ever since the invention of cellulose fibres, finding handmade paper had become a most arduous task. Celal had paid American and European brokers a pretty penny to buy up the paper stock that was left over from the local factory, which had closed down twenty-five years earlier. But he wasn't picky when it came to pens. It was his belief that when someone reads a letter, the paper is what matters. People are swayed by how the paper feels, not how it looks, and in his mind ink was but a trifling matter.

Karachiyano Efendi,

Commonplace arguments only bruise the honour of the weak. The fact of the matter is that I cannot rectify this situation by apologizing to you. Nor would sending you to your maker set things right. You see, apologies cannot instil in a man a robust sense of honour, which in most cases is a characteristic produced at birth. The only solution for you is to be born again of firmer stuff. I would like to kindly request that you awake from your delusions. A matter concerning a defect of birth cannot be solved with a bullet or the blow of a sword.

Yours truly, Celal Bey

*

Arif Bey was perhaps the wealthiest man in Manisa. He had made a fortune exporting the figs, grapes and olives that grew on his estate, shipping them as far afield as France and Italy. A gentleman of fine tastes, he was fond of reading and writing. He was a reserved man, as quiet as they come.

After losing his wife in a boating accident, he sold off part of his business. When that wild boy came into his life, Arif Bey straightened him out by arranging private lessons for him. Celal was steadfastly loyal to Arif Bey, who had saved him from a bedraggled life of living on the run and working in the slaughterhouse, up to his ears in animal intestines. Until then, Celal had never felt loyal to anyone. Arif Bey's generosity, which blew into Celal's life like a gentle breeze, changed all that.

Thanks to his governesses and the lessons he was given, Celal quickly outlearnt the other children of his age. Encouraged by Arif Bey's friends from France, he went to high school in Marseille, where he worked at the company's local branch, learning about the export trade. When Celal had completed his bachelor's degree with honours, Arif Bey summoned his adoptive son to Istanbul and enrolled him in the newly founded School of Law.

After settling back into Arif Bey's mansion in Istanbul, Celal found that he was confronted with a quietude that grew heavier with each passing day. The joy that Celal had brought into Arif Bey's life pulled the merchant, even if just a little, from the well of melancholy into which he'd fallen, but it didn't take long for him to plummet back into its depths.

Still wracked with pain over the loss of his wife, one day at dawn Arif Bey went to the neighbourhood of Bebek. Generously tipping the beardless owner of a rowing boat, he set off by himself, rowing straight towards a mail ship that was approaching the docks in Karaköy. The mail ship may have been old but it wasn't so decrepit that it couldn't pulverize the tiny craft in an instant. As Arif Bey was drowning, it occurred to him that perhaps he should have given the owner of the rowing boat a more sizeable tip.

Devastated by the fact that he'd been unable to console Arif Bey and that he'd lost his adoptive father, Celal dropped out of the School of Law, which he'd been attending solely out of a sense of devotion, and went on living in the mansion, which he now owned, together with two servants.

As the result of a few unwise investments, Celal lost a large part of his inheritance, but that didn't quite spell disaster because he still had a means of making money which was, to say the least, anything but ordinary. One day, after sending one of his servants to the Italian consulate to deliver a missive, he sat down at his desk for a light meal and then took a rather ordinary piece of paper from one of the drawers and started writing.

He was picking up from where he'd left off working on a novel. But this was not your typical novel. It was one of those notoriously popular French erotic books, the kind that was strictly forbidden yet read in secret by students, corporals, generals and parliamentarians alike. They would clandestinely meet up to slip each other the volumes they'd finished reading in exchange for others.

In France, the police were searching high and low for the author of these novels that depicted the harems of sultans, garrulous nights of drinking at caravanserais, women's sheer face veils, and gowns that fluttered in the breeze. Their efforts, however, were in vain.

For nothing the police hauled in and beat up a journalist who wrote about the Eastern Question.

At the Sorbonne they raided the office of a renowned Orientalist, leaving his library in a state of complete disarray, but it was an exercise in futility.

They interrogated a naval captain who was infatuated with Istanbul, and while they didn't learn anything useful they did come upon some unthinkably perverse gadgets at his home.

Celal sent the manuscripts he wrote to Jean, a high-school friend who was living in Marseille.

The French clerk on the mail ship was paid off so he'd overlook the parcels. The books were then sent section by section to five different addresses in Paris, where they were compiled at a printing shop set up expressly for that purpose in the basement of a photography studio. The Assistant Commissioner working at the police station next door didn't object to the opportunity to use the basement to question prostitutes a few times a week.

Celal was the secret driving force behind a booming industry. Aside from Jean, no one knew about Celal's role in the business. When he was a student in Marseille, he had started writing the stories for fun and as a way to earn some spending money. Now, while he didn't really need the money, he was making a small fortune from the books he wrote. At the time, however, Istanbul was crawling with Sultan Abdulhamid's spies, so if sizeable amounts of money were sent to a bank account there, someone was inevitably going to catch on. So Jean kept the money in an account in France and sent Celal modest amounts of money that wouldn't draw the attention of the authorities.

When Celal had finished writing a scene in which he described how some odalisques managed to rouse the manhood of the harem eunuchs, he looked at his watch. He knew that the French mail ship would still be going through all the rigmarole necessary to leave port. The French weren't just exporting their fashions and language to the Ottoman Empire, but their procedures and bureaucracy as well. There were so many formalities that they had to stop loading the ship two hours before it was due to depart, because that was how long it took to take care of all the forms, stamps and signatures.

After finishing another scene involving a eunuch and two odalisques fawning over the sultan's favourite mistress, Celal folded up the pages and placed them in a large envelope. He had been writing non-stop, and dawn was now breaking. Getting to his feet, he stretched and considered taking a quick nap. When he realized that he only had an hour to deliver the envelope, however, he hurriedly dressed and rushed out. As he quickly walked in the direction of the docks, he thought, "I wonder if it would have been better if the sultan's mistress had been bowing and scraping before the eunuch?"

Just as he was passing Kılıç Ali Pasha Mosque, Karachiyano stepped into Celal's path. At first, Celal didn't recognize him. It was only when Karachiyano threw a glove at his feet that he recalled who he was. Celal didn't refrain from showing his displeasure at the persistence of this particular Christian Istanbulite.

Without batting an eye, Celal picked up the glove and stuffed it into his pocket, and then continued on his way to deliver his story about the odalisques and eunuch to the post office clerk. He picked up the money that had been sent and saw that Jean had shipped him a rather large parcel. While he couldn't wait to open it, he knew that he couldn't do so until he got home. Part of the reason why Celal was somewhat obsessed with the pictures that accompanied his novels was the fact that the artist was a woman. Celal sometimes gazed at the pictures, running his fingers over them, and sometimes he scrutinized them with a magnifying glass. He wondered if the artist had included pictures of herself in some of her illustrations. If so, which one was she? For days Celal would be plunged into thought, pondering over the pictures. Celal created the female characters and the artist drew what he imagined. Over time, he started to notice the characters whom he hadn't described in sufficient detail. That woman, who piqued his interest more than any other, was somehow able to create drawings that filled in the gaps in Celal's descriptions. And it occurred to Celal that anyone who can do that must always draw their inspiration from themselves. Eventually Celal started trying to get the artist to draw a portrait of herself. Every story that he sent to France had one character who was described in only the vaguest of terms. He would, for example, leave out a description of a woman's nipples, and then he would take note of how she had drawn them. Sometimes he would fail to include a description of a woman's hair, or he would offer only the briefest rendering of a woman's eyes, lips or hands.

When the artist joined in the game, Celal raised the stakes. For example, he wrote a scene in which a Circassian odalisque climaxes, but he left the description rather bland. When the illustrated book arrived in the post a month later, he looked through it to see how she had depicted the woman's climax. He had written scenes in which fear, compassion, betrayal, admiration, disappointment and passion were all roughly sketched out, certain that the author and artist were winking at each other through their work. He had good reason to be more excited about this package than the others. In his last novel he had included a woman who was an artist, so he felt certain that he was going to come face to face with the woman of his imagination.

As he approached the mansion, the afternoon call to prayer was echoing through the streets. When he got to his room, he ripped open the package and started flipping through the pages. He found the illustration he was looking for at the back of the book. The drawing depicted an artist's studio. A woman was lying sprawled out on a canvas that had fallen to the floor and a man had his face buried between her legs. The woman was looking out of the drawing, as if gazing into Celal's eyes. Minutes went by, and they gazed at each other. Celal climaxed.

When Celal got up a few hours later he was feeling groggy. He left the copy of his latest book—which, as usual, he had written under the pseudonym Şerif Efendi—on the bed and sat down at his desk. He opened a thickly bound tome he had picked up from his office and found the page that his friend, a lawyer, had marked. Out loud he read the decree of Yako Sami, a member of the Ionian Court of First Instance:

"Duelling contravenes the fundamentals of our religious law. The body belongs to the earth, and the soul belongs to God the Almighty. Hence the body shall not be made to suffer death until so decreed by the Powers Above. Any order that condemns the body to death contravenes the principles of religion and hence is *haram*."

Celal knew most of this already, but it set his mind at ease to see that a scholar had expressed the claim so concisely. He lingered on one sentence in particular: "Hence the body shall not be made to suffer death..." To allow oneself to be killed was the equivalent of suicide, and so duelling itself was a form of suicide. And since suicide was forbidden by Islam, duelling was also forbidden. Therefore it seemed to stand that no one, least of all Karachiyano, could proclaim a duel and thereby force a Muslim to sin in the capital city of the Ottoman Empire. If the duel were to involve two non-Muslims, well that would be a different matter. Perhaps the police or the courts could turn a blind eye. Celal thought,

"But what would happen if the duel involved a Muslim? No, it simply wouldn't be tolerated." He flipped through some more pages, seeking arguments that would further strengthen his case. Even though he knew his argument was sound, he went through his bookshelves to find a philosophical and moral defence for his position. After going through book after book, he came across a pamphlet written by İsmail Hakkı Bey from the province of Milas. As he read through the pamphlet, Celal jotted down some notes:

"Do the insults and injustices that precipitate a duel represent circumstances that perforce lead to the death or killing of a person? These insults and injustices are, for the most part, unclear in nature. It is often said that honour demands blood. But what honour is this? We have seen that honour consists in not heeding such matters and paying heed to oneself. A sense of honour steeped in morality rises above the claims of others. So in the full sense, the act of securing my honour can only be carried out by me; no one else can exalt, disparage or eradicate it. Only I can disparage it with my mistakes and exalt it with my innate competence. If I err in my acts, a duel will not set them right; by taking part in a duel, I will only add injustice to an iniquity, and my sullied honour will not be cleansed."

An article titled "Duelling: One-On-One Combat" in the journal *Penman* further supported Celal's position:

"The tradition thus mentioned is a carry-over from the forefathers of the inhabitants of Germania, a remnant of their nomadic lifestyle and ignorance. In times of yore, the peoples of Europe were bereft of any form of judiciary process or governance and hence they resorted to duelling to settle disputes between people when they arose."

Celal penned a lengthy letter to Karachiyano which spelt out every reason why duelling was not a viable solution. He had never felt such passion before, not even when he was writing about the odalisques in his novel.

As Karachiyano would see that evening when he received the twenty-five-page letter, duelling simply was not an option. First of all, it went against the principles of Islam. Secondly, it is impossible for one person to sully the honour of another. Third, there were other ways to settle disputes. In the end, Celal challenged his adversary to a wrestling match.

"If you accept my proposal, we can thus satisfy your desire and engage in *corps-à-corps* combat while not indulging in behaviour that would run counter to my beliefs. The first man to be pinned to the ground shall vow to leave the city and keep his promise."

In this way, Celal managed to convince Karachiyano to drop his challenge. In trying to save himself, Celal had invoked the spirit of the day and age: he was Islamicized and Turkified, and as such he was a man of the times. He was not, however, Turkified to the extent that they would wrestle in the classic Turkish style, doused in olive oil, nor was he Europeanized to the extent that they would wrestle on mats. No, they would have a simple wrestling match following the *karakucak* tradition. They agreed to hold the match two weeks later.

The dervish lodges dedicated to wrestling had closed down long ago, and the instructors of times past had largely been forgotten. When the Military School was opened, wrestling was abandoned in favour of gymnastics, and traditional wrestlers were forced to eke out a living by taking part in competitions held at fairs in distant rural towns. Celal managed to track down a few wrestlers who had once trained at a lodge in the district of Şişli in Istanbul. He summoned them to the local hammam and, generously tipping the homeless boys working there, requested that the proprietor not disturb them. For days he tussled with the wrestlers at the bathhouse, learning how to fend off the most powerful of moves. Despite years of carousing, he hadn't lost an ounce of the strength that had once made it possible for him to fell a bull with a single blow. The head of the wrestling lodge had died long ago, but Celal picked up the seasoned wrestlers' secrets with astonishing speed and his spirits were buoyed by his successes. On the last two days he called musicians to the hammam, including a drummer and player of the *shawm*. They danced the *köroğlu zeybeği* and slapped their thighs before rushing in to grapple as the music played. Standing as tall and strong as obelisks on the marble platform in the middle of the bathhouse, which had been greased to make it all the more difficult for them to keep their balance, they eyed their opponents, watching for an opportunity to lunge and take them down. When evening fell, Celal's servants brought roast chicken, beef rump, Uzbek rice and Bosnian pastries. Some of the wrestlers guzzled iced pitchers of buttermilk *ayran* while others relaxed with a few strong glasses of raki.

On the day of the match Celal awoke before dawn feeling sprightly and alert. Heeding the advice of the wrestlers, he had a light breakfast: a few olives, a piece of bread and a glass of water. The day before he had told his driver to pick him up early, and he was waiting outside with the carriage. They immediately set off, first down the cobbled streets of Beyoğlu and then jolting along the narrow lanes towards Baltalimanı Meadow, where they had agreed to meet.

Karachiyano was already there, waiting beside a carriage similar to Celal's. He called out to Celal, "Welcome, wrestler, don your wrestling trousers! But let's have a smoke first, before settling this matter." Celal saw that there were two hookah pipes on the ground next to Karachiyano's carriage.

"By all means, Karachiyano Efendi. But may I ask the reason why?"

"Well, we're not going to have a duel, so we're both going to come out of this alive. That's something worthy of a celebration. Before, we were going to battle it out like enemies—now we're going to spar like comrades. We could even say that this is a gesture of peace. It is said that the natives of America smoke a peace pipe to settle disputes. And a little while from now I might be lying flat on my back on the grass, bidding farewell to this city, so please indulge me and allow me the pleasure of a last smoke with you."

The two young men sitting there bare-chested, wearing nothing but their canvas trousers as they puffed away at their water pipes, were likely a strange sight. After a few more puffs, Karachiyano set his hose on the ground and got to his feet, and Celal followed suit. Half-heartedly they went through the routine of slapping their thighs before lunging in for the attack. Every move that Karachiyano made betrayed inexperience. All Celal wanted was to get through the ordeal and go back home, but just as he grabbed his opponent by the back of the neck and heard the man's bones crack under his grip, hundreds of flies swarmed over him. And not just any flies, but the biting kind. Some landed on his shoulders and feet, while others buzzed in his face, biting his ears and nose. Taking advantage of Celal's bewilderment, Karachiyano made his move.

Celal could hardly open his eyes. The swarm of flies was getting thicker with each passing second, flying in for the attack again each time that Karachiyano let go. A rat scurried through the grass towards Celal and started snapping at his feet. Celal bellowed, scratching at the swarm of creatures attacking him. He felt as though the flies were trying to burrow into his ears, and he started pounding his head against the damp ground. So sure was he that the rat had gnawed off his entire left foot that he didn't even realize that he was lying on his back.

"It is said that the natives in America smoke a peace pipe to settle disputes." True, and they also sprinkled dried angel's trumpet into the tobacco and drove the white man mad... The rat vanished, and the flies, too, were disappearing.

"If you can't win with your fists, use your wits. A trick is only a trick if you're already strong enough to win in a brawl." Süleyman had said that. And he was right. Of course he was right. That's why he had the best pocket knife around. If he hadn't deserved it, the big boys would've taken it away.

As Karachiyano was circling around him, Celal muttered: "Rat, rat, this is what you get / We'll throw you from the minaret / There's a bird up there with silvery wings / And uncle's pockets are full of shiny things."

3

Checkmate!

I T WAS JUST A CHEST. A wooden chest, covered in travel stickers that had been varnished over, becoming one with the surface, albeit with some difficulty you could still make out the names of ship and train companies. Celal stared at it, still disorientated.

It was just a wooden chest. A hefty old chest. Then again, all chests come into the world at a ripe old age and with a ponderous appearance. You'd never expect the handles on the sides to start flapping, or for the chest to take to the air.

Candelabra, on the other hand, can suddenly take flight, flitting here and there despite their weight. That is, except for those in churches.

As for vases, people always want to pour their woes into them, especially if they have broad mouths. At the bottom of such vases, words circle around, chasing their tails like trapped fish.

A good chair should resemble a colt standing on trembling legs. Most of the time they do. That's why people sitting on chairs think differently from people sitting on settees.

It was just an old wooden chest. No candelabra, vases or chairs would be packed inside it. The masterfully crafted bookcase, the bed with its ornate headboard, the bed sheets, the water scoop at the hammam and the marble-covered walls of the hall would all stay just where they were.

Shame cannot be left at home. Nor can you lock it away. If you try to hide shame in a vase, any flowers you put in there will wither and die.

That feeling of shame will grunt and roar like a vicious gorilla. Trying to keep it quiet is one thing, but getting rid of it is quite another.

You have no choice but to fill your pockets with your shame and leave. You'll be so weighed down that all you'll be able to carry with you is an old wooden chest.

Plunged into thought, Celal was sitting on his bed with his feet placed on a wooden chest. Of course, he could have just shot Karachiyano. Or, if he'd told the men at the wrestling lodge what had happened, they would've taken matters into their own hands. But he couldn't go against what he'd believed in when he'd saved himself by pissing in the face of the shop owner. In the end, Karachiyano's trick was the work of a divine hand restoring the balance of things. Celal accepted what had happened as his fate and kept his word. Boarding a mail ship, the hull of which still bore the traces of bulls' horns and Arif's rowing boat, he left Istanbul, setting off down the Bosphorus strait like an ox fleeing a cloud of tormenting gadflies.

*

Throughout the journey Celal merely sat and stared at the ship's billowing smokestacks, hardly speaking a word to anyone.

It wasn't for naught that such vessels were called "steamships". The thick steam poured back over the cluttered deck and slowly dissipated into the blue of the sky and sea. Celal imagined himself suspended in that scalding cloud, and then his red-hot body plunging into the sea in a hissing puff of steam.

The trip was so tedious that he was almost pleased when the police took him into custody the moment he set foot on the wharf.

"Celal Bey, our ships are fast but telegrams are even faster. We were all pleasantly surprised to see your name on the passenger list. For a long time now we have been hoping that you would come, so this is a happy day for us. I know that this is nothing like the tobacco you have back home but please, help yourself."

From where he remained standing, Celal leant over to pick up the cigarette rolling towards him across the Commissioner's desk. He caught the match that the Commissioner tossed to him and lit the cigarette, taking a deep drag.

Gesturing to a chair, the Commissioner said, "Forgive my rudeness, please have a seat. First of all, let me say that I'm not really a fan of your work. But I'm certain that if I were to search the desks of the officers working at this station I'd be sure to find a few copies. Truly banal stuff. Wouldn't you say that it's degrading, in a way?"

Celal sat down.

"I hope that you won't be offended if I tell you that I have no idea what you're talking about," he said.

"Please, Celal, let's not deceive ourselves. It's clear that you're on a little vacation. The only thing preventing you from getting out of here and spending the night in your comfortable bed at your hotel in a way befitting the books you write is you. Believe me, the sooner that we can solve this dilemma, the better off we'll all be. You're probably wondering how we identified you, so let me explain it all so that you won't go on embarrassing yourself by denying the truth of the matter."

The Commissioner took off his jacket, hung it up, and lit a cigarette. After sitting back down, he went on: "I don't have a problem with the books you write. For twenty-six years I've been solving murders. I'm not concerned with banning your books just because a few priests don't like them. I truly couldn't care less. In any case, we brought you in for something that is far more important. I wish that I could give you good news. At the murder bureau, the best news we can give goes along the lines of 'Ma'am, we found your husband's murderer.' Those aren't the sort of glad tidings you deliver with bells ringing in your voice! 'Bells ringing in your voice'—that's rather good isn't it?... You see, I'd like to write a book of my own, but not the kind that you write. I'd like to try my hand at proper literature. The real thing. If I were to write about the murders I've solved, I'd have a complete oeuvre. These days newspapers publish novels in series. Which is fine, and they pay as well. But it's hard work. And then there's the matter of the proverbial grindstone. I just don't have the time. 'Bells ringing in your voice'... I'm fond of metaphors. What do you think? As matters stand, however, I'm not going to be able to write those books."

"Commissioner, please get to the point."

"Indeed, let me get to the point. Your pen pal, Jean..." He shuffled through some notes on his desk and went on: "Jean Vergez. He was killed on the same day you set out on your journey here. Shot in the head several times. Clearly it was a crime of passion. We searched his home in an attempt to find some clues and we found an envelope postmarked from Istanbul among his documents. It contained a chapter from one of Şerif Efendi's books. When we discovered that the chapter hadn't been published yet, it was a simple matter of putting two and two together: the notorious author was from Istanbul. There was no return address on the envelope, so we did some digging around to find out whether Jean had any Turkish acquaintances and we came across your name. The two of you studied at the same high school. By a happy coincidence, you decided to fulfil your longing to visit our country again, and so here we are. It's quite simple, isn't it?"

Celal listened coolly to the news of Jean's death. After being duped by Karachiyano, he had been expecting that everything would take a turn for the worse. He had even hoped it would. His gaze lingered on the floor. The parquet was buckling up along the edge of the carpeting, rounding into curves that began to take on the shape of a dog's head that undulated along the floor until it reached Celal's foot, where it looked up at him and sadly winked. As the Commissioner hoarsely went on speaking, the mournful dog's head suddenly deflated like a balloon.

Celal replied, "It truly is simple. *Primo*, and may God Almighty forgive your error, you have no proof that the person who sent Jean that envelope was me. *Secundo*, no connection can be made between me and Şerif Efendi's books. *Tertio*, let's suppose that I did write the books and was sending them to Jean. You are not an officer of the moral police, so you have no right to intervene. And, since I was in another country when the murder was committed, you cannot charge me with anything. The simplicity of a matter does not mean that the analysis or solution will be simple as well. As a clever, experienced detective you should know that better than anyone else."

The Commissioner silently got to his feet and walked over to the coat stand. He grabbed his jacket and stood there for a moment, deep in thought. Then he walked towards the door and, with his back to Celal, said, "Quite right, sir. I do not have the right to detain you. But there is a very good restaurant just down the street. If you'll allow me, I'll have your chest sent to a nearby hotel where you can relax after we've dined. But you will be my guest, and I won't accept any objections."

The restaurant had a few long tables that were arranged in rows. It was an unremarkable place, the kind frequented by labourers, petty officers and poor students. There was a common belief that such restaurants always had at least one dish that outshone the food served in the finest restaurants, but Celal was in no mood for such trivialities; so he ordered steak with mashed potatoes, while the Commissioner asked for two boiled eggs. They drank the house wine, which was served up in pitchers set out on the tables.

Twirling his moustache, the Commissioner looked at the eggs that were brought to him. First he cut one of the eggs in half and then into quarters, and then he sprinkled it with pepper. After draining his glass in a single gulp, he popped one of the quarters of egg into his mouth. He chewed it for a moment and then, still rolling the egg around in his cheek, said, "I know who you are. If I so desired, I could have you arrested for the books you write and get back to work on the murder case. But in doing so, I would incur your animosity, which is the last thing I want, because I'd like to work with you on something…"

Celal took a sip of wine, which was so sour that it seared his tongue, and nodded for the Commissioner to go on.

"We have evidence proving that you are the writer who goes by the pen name Şerif Efendi. I hope you realize that we wouldn't launch an investigation based on an envelope without a return address. That was just a clue. And what good is a clue if it doesn't lead anywhere? Of course, as you know the word for 'clue' in Turkish means the end of a piece of thread—the idea behind the metaphor being that if you follow the thread, it will lead you back to the beginning. Naturally, I don't speak your language. But you see, I have a certain occupational illness that has led me to become fascinated by the etymology of the word 'clue' in particular tongues. Let me confess that I take notes on such matters, as one day I will write my own books. In French, the word for 'clue' is *indice*. It comes from the Latin word meaning 'to point'. So we followed the thread of the clue in your language and looked where it pointed."

With his tongue Celal was trying to dislodge a piece of gristle stuck between his teeth. The way that the Commissioner seemed to be bluffing, yet revealing critical details at the same time, made him uneasy.

"In that case, sir, you should have tied that thread around your finger. I fear you may have forgotten what you were really looking for."

Celal was surprised when the Commissioner appeared to be pleased by what he'd said.

42

"The fact that you appear calm but are behaving so impatiently is sufficient proof that you indeed are Şerif Efendi. You like irony. We all do. Do you know what sarcasm is? Please forgive my pedantry, it's only natural that a fan of literature like myself would be somewhat pedantic in the presence of a writer. The word 'sarcasm' comes from the Greek *sarkazein*, which means 'to strip meat from the bone'. Just like you've been trying to do for the last five minutes with that steak which is as tough as leather. The steak here used to be much better.

"In any case, I had you brought into the police station to warn you that the things you've written under the pen name Şerif Efendi could land you in serious trouble. I hope you are aware of the fact that it is not customary in my country to drink wine with people who are suspected of having committed a crime."

"Commissioner, I can only hope that your fascination with literature hasn't blinded you to certain hard facts. Maybe you have just created a fantasy for yourself as a means of coping with the murders you've been dealing with for so many years."

The Commissioner downed another glass of wine and set about meticulously cutting up the other egg. "That's possible," he said. "When you spend so much time in the murder business, you start wanting to destroy yourself little by little. But unfortunately your theory doesn't apply to the case at hand. Although it would be nice to finish off my career by getting lost in such exotic fantasies.

"Monsieur Celal, I am a meticulous man! I take my job seriously. I didn't just follow up on the trail of a letter that arrived from Istanbul so that I could see where it would lead me. Your friend Jean was very scrupulous about his private affairs. We were unable to find anything worthy of note concerning his love life. But all the signs were pointing with the fixity of a compass at his pocketbook."

Celal stopped mashing his lumpy potatoes with his fork.

The Commissioner went on: "We looked into his bank accounts but didn't find anything out of the ordinary. Then we came upon a joint account. The other holder of the account, an Ottoman subject, was none other than Celal, son of Arif. It would seem that you are a respected figure. That's why I told you up front not to embarrass yourself by denying the truth of the matter. Checkmate! Or, in Pashto, *shāh māt*: 'The king is helpless.'"

Celal called the waiter over. Huffing and puffing, the pot-bellied waiter squeezed his way between the tables and approached. Celal handed him some money and asked him to fetch a bottle of the finest champagne from the wine shop a few streets down, as he knew that the only region that hadn't been affected by the recent blight was Champagne.

4

The Winged Bats are Right

"JEAN,
Bank,
Fake Celal,
Murder."

Two bottles of the finest champagne, after some rather uninspiring Burgundy. Steak and mashed potatoes. The eggs that the Commissioner rolled around on his plate. Cigarettes lit one after the other.

The champagne, however, was actually quite good. Toasting disasters with champagne was a proper way to resign oneself to fate. But still, Celal thought as he sat in his hotel room, we should be grateful for what we have...

Celal was rocking back and forth in his chair, making it squeak with increasing rapidity, and occasionally glancing at the notes he'd made on a small piece of paper. Jean had been murdered. Two days before he was killed, he had gone to the bank with someone and withdrawn all the money from the joint account. The bank manager had known Jean for a long time so he hadn't been suspicious. The passport that was presented by the man introduced as Celal seemed genuine. The age, height and description of the passport bearer were indicated in the document, and the Police Commissioner said that the description of the person who presented it was a perfect match. The passport picture was blurry, as was usual, and in any case bearded Ottoman men tended to look the same.

The small fortune that Celal had been hiding from Sultan Abdul Hamid's spies was gone.

First of all, they had killed Jean. Then there was the matter of the bank account.

Using a red pen, he connected the words in his notes with lines:

Jean—Bank—Fake Celal—Murder.

As the moustached Commissioner had said, his life could be in grave danger. But no matter how hard he tried, he couldn't understand what had happened. Slowly he started folding the piece of paper into a crane. As would be expected of a paper crane, it tried to stand up on its twig-like legs. After taking a few steps, it tremulously took to the air. When the crane slammed into the window, which was partially open, it plummeted to the ground.

Celal picked the crane up and placed it on a small silver tray on the table. Pulling the last match from his pocket, he set the tip of one of its wings on fire. The crane suddenly straightened up and then burst into flames.

Taking a deep breath, Celal scattered the crane's ashes

around the room, muttering, "When you're in a pinch, put your faith in the elements. Earth, water, wind, fire…"

The first thing Celal did was buy a ticket back to Istanbul, which left him with little money. The next morning, as he was going through his chest, he came across a thin notebook. A note written by the Commissioner was attached to it: "This is the draft of a book written by a close friend of mine who is an aspiring writer. When you get a chance, I'd appreciate it if you could take a look." Celal weighed the notebook in his hand, thinking that it was probably a sly attempt by the Commissioner to show Celal his own work. In the end, he decided to take it with him as he left the hotel.

He stopped at a café up the street after a quick shave and then started walking the streets of the city, a few times running the risk of getting lost to make sure that no one was following him. As he walked, sweat started pouring down his face, stinging his freshly shaven cheeks, so he sat down on a park bench for a while before continuing on his way. At one point he stopped to eat a generously buttered ham sandwich at the end of a cul-de-sac and then clambered over two walls to throw himself into the throng of people bustling along the next street. After dusk had fallen, he continued his peregrinations in the outskirts of Marseille. The sky was clear and the air was balmy, so he decided to sleep on a pile of hay near a vineyard abutting a farmhouse.

When Celal awoke with the morning sun shining in his eyes, he saw a servant step out of a nearby hut. Calling him over, Celal offered to buy an old horse he'd seen tied up near the farmhouse. The deal done, Celal squeezed his swollen feet into his shoes and swung himself into the saddle, and although the horse was as listless as they come Celal set off with the decisiveness of Don Quixote, riding the old horse as far as it could go—which was the first station on the train line from Marseille to Paris.

After setting the horse free when a train bound for Paris pulled into the station a few hours later, Celal boarded the train and settled into a seat, noting that it was almost completely empty. Like everyone who enjoys travelling by rail, he gazed out of the window, watching the scenery speed by, and then felt an urge to read something. He took the notebook that the Commissioner had slipped into his chest from his bag. The first thing that he noticed was that it was written in Turkish. Intrigued, he started reading:

ARIF BEY, THE WINGED BATS ARE RIGHT

—A One-Act Play in Four Scenes—

SCENE ONE

The courtyard of Arif's home. A path lined with fruit trees leads to the garden wall. Mount Sipylus fills the horizon in all its majesty. There are a desk and a chair in the courtyard.

The afternoon call to prayer has just resounded from the minaret of the nearby mosque. Darkness is starting to fall. Arif and Pierre are in deep conversation as they walk among the fruit trees.

PIERRE (*pulling a tree branch laden with apples towards him, he plucks one of the apples from the branch and, holding it to the bridge of his nose, examines it closely, one eye closed*) Take the worm in this apple, for instance. Did nature want this apple to be riddled with holes or does the worm exist so that we'll have to learn how to deal with such things? (*He bites into the apple*) Maybe it's the same thing. An affliction, a calamity, has been unleashed upon us and I'm trying to fend it off. Call it what you will—God, nature, it doesn't matter. Regardless of whoever or whatever brought it upon us, there is a cure. There is a cure that we can track down, dazzling it with a torch in its lair and then pulling it out by its ear.

ARIF (*gazing at the mountain*) Do you really believe that the remedy is hidden in that mountain?

PIERRE It's not hidden. You can't hide a mountain, can you? Your mountain there is drawing iron towards itself. Even if you could hide the mountain, you couldn't hide the iron. The remedy has left its traces out in the open. And what's out in the open for all to see is destiny. As the human mind works to achieve its destiny, everything acquires meaning, and in the process we become one with our fate. And what is destiny? A pointless weed growing in nature's garden? A path chosen by God? It's not that important. When you become one with your destiny, you either arrive at nature or attain that which is divine. Or maybe both at the same time…

Pierre takes Arif by the arm and they slowly start walking towards the house.

ARIF (*plunged into thought*) These days I've been thinking a lot about death. Actually, I'm not even sure that "death" is the right word. It's more like I've been thinking about what happens after death. I'm concerned, but not about what will happen to my poor soul. The body isn't the prison of the soul. Ever since I understood that saying such a thing isn't a sin, I've been more at ease. In reality the soul is the prison of the body. You mentioned attaining that which is divine, and you were right. The soul was breathed into us… Meaning that the source of the soul is the divine. The soul prevents the body from attaining its desires, which means that this is what God Almighty wants. Life isn't difficult. It's enough if you discipline the body with that which the divine has breathed into the soul.

Silence.

PIERRE (*trying to be convincing*) The divine or nature… Our woes and the remedy are the very essence of our souls. Until the day of death, the soul speaks to us of that which is relevant. But the soul can't always stifle the body's desires. No matter how much you control your-self, there's always a chance that at one point you'll find yourself in a situation in which the soul breaks down. In fact, that which belongs to the body consists of the blink of an eye. If the body deceives the soul but once, you can then dupe it with a single reality. After a while, you start thinking that what you've grown accustomed to, that which you've seen, are rules that have been laid down by the soul. But the things to which we are accus-tomed are just the stringing together of the moments of the body's blink of an eye. (*Excitedly*) Think about it like this. You look up and see a bird flap its wings once. You look again, and yet again you see the bird flap its wings. Then when you see the bird flapping its wings with every blink of your eye, you notice that it is flying. However, the things to which you're accustomed are not the true basis of perception. Sure, the bird is flying, but not because someone looked at it or because you're used to looking at it. The bird is flying because every muscle in its wings has been designed for that. The bird is flying not because someone has watched it fly but because someone observed it and made measured observations of *how* it flies. The signs are there for all to see. But if the human mind does not seek out those signs, the divine order or the laws of nature cannot be grasped. And when they are not grasped, the bird flies for nothing. It's just you watching a bird, nothing more or less.

ARIF (*animatedly*) Did the Absolute Being create birds just
so they could be dissected with the aim of understanding how they fly? What good will it do anyone, if they
find out how a bird flies without comprehending *why*
it flies?

PIERRE (*emphatically*) Arif Bey, it will do plenty of good. (*He
stops and with a grand gesture points to the mountain*) Just like
with your mountain there, drawing iron into itself. The
way that the mountain attracts iron is a sign in itself. It's
a riddle put in place by divine fate, by nature, for us to
solve. And when we solve it, we may not understand *why*
it does that. We don't understand why birds fly when
we work out how they fly. That's not the problem. If we
can comprehend the "how", we can then be part of the
remedy of the "why". (*Silence*) I know that I've rambled
on a lot but there's something about the shadow of that
mountain, it says something. (*They walk in silence*) I was
listening to you… You were saying that you were thinking
about what happens after death.

ARIF (*takes a deep breath*) I'm not too worried about the salvation of my soul. I've soundly imprisoned my body in my
soul. (*Concerned*) Of course, we all know who is up above
and, who knows, perhaps I deserve to be punished far
worse than the most wicked of sinners… (*Agitated*) Still,
I know that I have done everything I could for the grace
of God. And I know that even saying such a thing is a
sin. But I can't stop myself! There are people who have

never fallen prey to anger or passion. They always take shelter in logic, in understanding. Such people simply observe humanity because they think that, in doing so, they can then distinguish between God and superstition. As they tread down God's path, they hold to the false belief that they are following reason, and as they drink of its narcissistic tranquillity they think that they have turned their back on superstition. But the thing is, when they prattle on about being sensible, and stability, they don't realize how misguided they actually are. (*Sadly*) So, Monsieur Pierre, the whole lot of such people will fade away to death, struck down by an unknown ailment. Even so, their deaths will make sense to the people around them. And because they never glowed with life, the way they fade isn't really a fading at all. When they're gone, no one will say that they were on the side of God, that they rejected superstition. At best, someone might say, "He was a good person." That's it and nothing more.

PIERRE (*pauses mid-stride*) There are a thousand and one ways to take God's side against superstitions! But there's just one true path: embracing destiny in our very souls. It's in our power to establish the soul's reign over the body. Arif Bey, why does a murderer kill? Because his nature commands it or because his surroundings lead him to the act, right? His family, upbringing, income, education, and so on. The coming together of uncountable factors caused by a thousand and one reasons under certain conditions. (*A pause*) If he committed murder because his very nature drove him to do it, there's no way it could've been prevented. If the fault lies with his surroundings, it would be possible to identify what led him to do it and perhaps find a way to prevent it from happening again, but there is no single solution that would work for every society, every country, every age or every person. So tell me this, Arif Bey. What is our fate? To accept the fact that people kill one another or to find a way to prevent it? (*He smiles, noticing that Arif is listening carefully to his every word*) If you embrace your fate, you will never have to worry about being one of those people who simply fade away and die. Life is a game, Arif Bey. The person who embraces their fate understands the goal of the game. And when you do that, the horror of death vanishes. To do anything else is to lose the game, and the meaning of life wilts away. That's why people are so afraid of death. Perhaps it is actually quite easy to find one's fate and stave off the fear of death. So, let me ask you this: will you help me build the peace machine?

The sound of the call to prayer. Pierre offers Arif an apple.

ARIF (*hesitantly biting into the apple*) Monsieur Pierre, obviously you're not the only person waiting for an answer. (*He looks up at the sky*) I'm going to say my prayers now. That's when the best answers come to me.

The sun has set behind Mount Sipylus. Arif and Pierre are having dinner in the living room. Young Sahir is sitting at a desk in the courtyard working by the light of a candle. The desk is covered in papers.

ARIF (*glancing at Sahir*) In his own way, he's even sort of charming. And I wouldn't be off the mark if I said that he was intelligent. That's why I teach him things when I can find the time. Sometimes he cleaves right through the most difficult subjects as if he has a forehead like an ice-breaker, quickly learning by rote things that it would take someone like me an hour to learn. Of course, he's got his odd moods. Such a tenuous strangeness… Sometimes he doesn't hear what's said around him. He's got something feline like that in him—he suddenly gets spooked by things that I can't even see. Most of the time he just stays at home. Since his sensitive eyes aren't strained by the dim light, he works in the courtyard with a single candle, from the last prayer of the day until morning. I let him, so that he can get some fresh air. He does the accounts for my olive groves.

PIERRE Is he a good bookkeeper?

ARIF (*proudly*) He's extraordinary. As long as he's allowed to work after the sun goes down, he's proving to be a clever, efficient clerk. That is, if you know how to manage him.

Whoever he works for has to put up with his somewhat bizarre ways and frail constitution.

PIERRE (*popping stewed apricots into his mouth with pleasure; he pauses to wipe his moustache*) Has a doctor taken a look at his eyes?

ARIF Of course. An Italian doctor in Istanbul ascribed it to a neural disorder, saying that his nervous system is like a rowing boat in a storm. Like you, that particular doctor is well-versed in matters of electricity. He said that the tissue behind the lenses of Sahir's eyes is like wool cloth constantly being rubbed together, creating static electricity whenever he gets agitated.

PIERRE (*trying to remember something*) I think it's called... photophobia. An excessive build-up of electricity in the optic nerve. Such an unfortunate affliction. (*He pauses for a moment*) Why can't he go back to his village?

ARIF It's a rather odd place.

PIERRE (*suddenly interested, he glances at Sahir*) What's so strange about it?

ARIF (*reaching into his pocket, he pulls out a cigarette case; he offers Pierre a cigarette; a moment of silence*) As you know, we don't have lords, counts, dukes and marquises like you do in your country. We have agas, beys and pashas... But you won't find any of those in Sahir's village. They are simple folk. For the most part they are Muslim, but they don't like the people in the surrounding Greek villages because they're "newcomers". They disdain the Ottomans, too, saying that they're latecomers to the land. For them, even the prophet Abraham was a new arrival. If your lineage is known, then so is your name. For instance, all the men in Sahir's family are named Sahir. Every male child has to take up the same line of work as his father.

PIERRE (*putting out his cigarette*) So, why can't Sahir go back to his village?

ARIF Because his father was the village watchman, and also a hunter. With Sahir's eyes afflicted as they are, he can't do either.

PIERRE Isn't there any way that he can go back home?

ARIF Not really. You see, he ran away. The heads of all the families got together and declared him an outcast. There's a small stream called Red Brook which runs down the slope above the village. It is forbidden for anyone who has been cast out of the village to cross it again. But Sahir has little interest in going back. I've always been somewhat curious about the place, perhaps because I've heard so much about it. Sahir was just ten years old or so when he arrived in Manisa. A shopkeeper knew about my fascination with Kudretköy—which was the name of the village—so he told me about Sahir's arrival and I took him in. But Sahir refuses to even talk about Kudretköy. He's strange that way. Anyway… Pierre, I've put a lot of thought into this. But I have to confess, I can't quite grasp the particulars of those invisible sparks in the air and electromagnetism swaying the human mind. (*Murmuring to himself*) "His light is like a niche within which is a lamp, the lamp is within a glass bell, and the glass bell is a pearly white star." (*Speaking more loudly*) Still, my dear Monsieur Pierre, do you really think you can put an end to war?

PIERRE Most certainly. Haven't you noticed that all of our conversations keep coming back to the same point?

ARIF Peace?

PIERRE Exactly. Now, Arif Bey, let us work to realize our common dream. (*He gets to his feet*)

ARIF (*also rising to his feet*) Well said, Monsieur Pierre. But how?

PIERRE (*smiling, he places his hand on Arif's shoulder*) Now you, too, have come around to the question of "how". We're living in a new age, in a way that befits the times. We'll create a machine. A peace machine that will put an end to all wars.

SCENE THREE

Pierre and Arif are standing in a doorway that opens onto the garden. They are watching Sahir, who is still working at his desk at the far side of the courtyard.

ARIF A peace machine that will put an end to all wars… How is it going to work?

PIERRE (*turning his gaze from Sahir to Arif*) How do bats perceive the world around them, Arif Bey? By the sound of echoes. They hear an echo, and based on that they create an image in their minds. Because the sounds they make are actually waves, the images they create in their minds are in a constant state of motion. Arif Bey, bats are right. In the world, everything that seems still is actually moving all the time. Don't the verses in that holy book of yours say the same? "I created waves on the Earth so that all would be in fixed motion."

ARIF (*excitedly*) There are actually two verses. The other one says, "I placed great weights upon the Earth so that mankind would not be shaken and I raised stable mountains."

PIERRE *Voilà!* Some people fall from God's grace and struggle for years, yet in the end, like me, they become aware of certain things, seeing that what they've finally grasped has been winking at them all along in some holy text. Mountains weren't just put in place to anchor the ground during earthquakes. Some have their own unique functions.

ARIF You're talking about our mountain here, aren't you? The one that pulls in iron?

PIERRE (*smiling*) Yes. Just one of the many magnetic mountains. They regulate the magnetic order as the overseers of electromagnetism. The world wasn't created on a foundation of water or earth. Every single thing was built on electromagnetic waves. The Bible says, "In the beginning, God created the heavens and the earth. The earth was empty and formless, and darkness covered the vast expanse." (*He chuckles to himself. A few moments of silence*) Like the world, our souls are made of electromagnetic waves. But what seemed in the past to be a vast expanse covered in darkness is now visible to us. We are living in a day and age when the human race has discovered the essence of the universe. That was the task assigned to us. A question was asked and we found the answer through science.

ARIF (*as if reciting a prayer*) They say that the soul arises through the order of God but little of science has been granted you. (*Unsure of himself*) But—is that our task?

PIERRE By Jove, Arif Bey! I take my hat off to you. Erudition demands patience. If it were so easy to tell right from wrong, Eve wouldn't have eaten the apple simply because that's what the serpent told her to do. We are being tested, just as she was tested. The exhortation "Know thyself!" wasn't said in vain, nor was the injunction "Have the courage to use your reason." (*He pauses*) If only they'd all said, "Let's find solutions to the tasks set before us and answer the questions that face us in life." True, the soul is the work of God. But now we have science. We can make the soul carry out the commandments of God. (*Resolutely*) And could there be a more important divine order than creating peace in the world?

ARIF (*Unconvinced*) Monsieur Pierre, would you have poor Sahir, who is half-blind and such an odd character, carry out such a command?

PIERRE God works in mysterious ways and His judgements are inexplicable. Good and evil, compassion and cruelty—they all set up different vibrations in the soul. If we could measure those vibrations, we could create a peace machine capable of blocking those waves spread in the soul by wickedness and cruelty. And I believe that I can build it.

ARIF But are you sure that is the kind of task we should assign to a machine?

PIERRE Arif Bey, a machine is perfect for the job. Generation after generation of people have been living near this magnetic mountain, meaning that the vibration of their souls is more prominent than it is in others. And that's why some places have more saints and madmen than others. I kept thinking about that when you were telling me about Sahir and his village. Let me take Sahir with me to France, where I'll look after his education, and I'll also try to find a way to have his eyes treated. While there, I'll try to detect the vibrations of his soul. I assure you that not an ounce of harm will come to him. If perchance I am right, we will create the machine to establish everlasting peace. And if I'm wrong, that young man will still have a bright future before him. I promise you, I will look after him like my own son. Of course, he'll always be able to come back to you whenever he so desires.

5

The Hubris of Might

IT WASN'T SLEEPLESSNESS that was tying Celal's stomach in knots, but the play he'd been reading. As far as he knew, his adoptive father Arif Bey hadn't had any acquaintances by the name of Monsieur Pierre, nor had Celal ever heard of such a thing as a peace machine. As a child, Celal had gone to that house in Manisa and played in the courtyard described in the play. But he had never heard mention of anyone named Sahir.

Celal may not have been able to answer the questions swirling in his mind, but he knew it would be easy enough to find the printing house that published his books. He recalled that Jean had mentioned in his letters a photography studio, situated in one of those neighbourhoods that spiral out from the heart of Paris like the pattern on a snail's shell. Jean had said that they printed the books in the studio's basement, so Celal thought that if he spent the day wandering the streets of the neighbourhood he'd be able to find the place. When the train pulled into the station, Celal headed straight for the fifth arrondissement.

In no time at all he found the studio, but it turned out to be closed. In the shop window, which was covered in portraits and landscapes, Celal noticed a small handbill that had seemingly been taped to the glass more recently than the photographs.

Celal realized that the engraving on the handbill was the work of the woman who did the illustrations for his novels. It depicted a boy bringing his fist down on the head of a bull, and beneath the image was an address written in Arabic script, the same as the handwriting in the notebook he'd been reading. He took a mental note of the address, which consisted of three numbers and the name of a street: 227 rue de Vaugirard.

As Celal approached the address around noon, the back of his neck was damp with nervous sweat. He paused at the building's entrance and lit a cigarette, bile rising up in his throat as his heart beat wildly. As he considered resorting to tongue-twisters to pull himself together, an urge to flee bore down on him. Driven on, however, by a desire to see the woman who illustrated his books, he went in. A red carpet rose up a broad flight of stairs, held in place with brass fasteners. After pausing to catch his breath, he made his way up the stairs and then pressed the doorbell next to an oak door.

Like most men who find themselves standing on one side of a door separating them from a beautiful woman, Celal drew himself up to his full height and quickly brushed his hair with his hands, trying to make sure that his expression betrayed nothing but cool indifference. After a few moments, the heavy door swung open with a squeaky chuckle.

Celal found himself face to face with a slight, teary-eyed man in his fifties. The man nodded in greeting, and then pulled a cigar from the pocket of his straw-coloured silk jacket and lit it. Celal stood there, watching the man puff at the cigar to get it going. When he was satisfied that the cigar was properly lit, the man smiled and said, "My dear Celal Bey, your arrival has been eagerly anticipated. Please come in."

Celal hesitated for a moment. When the man briskly turned and started walking down the apartment's long entrance hall, Celal's curiosity won over his unease and he started to follow him. They arrived at a lavishly decorated living room. The man turned to Celal and said, "Please have a seat and relax. We have so much to talk about." He then walked over to the liquor cabinet and took out two crystal cognac glasses that gently clinked together. He filled the glasses and handed one of them to Celal, who had settled into the nearest chair.

"I was quite fond of your father, Celal."

Celal twirled the glass. The cognac swirled around the inside of the crystal and then slowly starting dripping back down in streaks. The light that managed to penetrate the heavy green velvet curtains gave the cognac a sickly hue. Celal rubbed his stubbly cheeks, unsettled by the darkness of the room. Smoke from the cigar drifted over his head, mingling with specks of dust floating in the air.

As Celal sat there silently, his host took a few sips from his glass. Celal took out the notebook and tossed it onto the table between him and the man.

"Sir, I was quite fond of my father as well. Now, would you mind if we opened the curtains?"

The man strode over to the window and pulled open the curtain. Riding the cool breeze, the scent of horse chestnuts drifted into the room through the half-open window.

"If perchance what you wrote is true, Sahir Bey, I would surmise, based on your handwriting and the moistness of your eyes, that Monsieur Pierre convinced my father to let him take you away."

Smiling briefly, the man said, "Sudden light. More than one truth… That's what your father would say when we drank until morning, the break of dawn taking us by surprise. Lightly punching my arm, he'd say, 'Get going, it's late.' He was a man of rituals. A poetic man."

After knocking back his drink in a single gulp, Celal took out a cigarette. Placing it in his mouth, he said, "The play you wrote has just one act and three scenes. I suppose you didn't have me come all the way here so that I could read the last scene, which seems to be missing."

Sahir took a handkerchief from his jacket pocket and wiped his eyes, which were a deep grey, like the fur of a smoke-coloured cat. Not bothering to hide his irritation, Celal went on: "You're the first person I've ever heard say that my father was a poet. Yes, he was a refined man, as gentlemanly as they come. But Sahir Bey, he wasn't the kind of man who would drink until morning. Once in a blue moon he would drink a small glass of orange liqueur with his coffee, but aside from that I never saw him touch alcohol."

"That's right, dear boy, he liked orange liqueur. He made it himself, didn't he? On such mornings he would always drink one glass before sending me off to sleep. Like I said, your father was a man of ritual. If you have the time, I'd like to tell you what I know about him."

Celal fixed his eyes on the window. Stirred by a light breeze, a branch of the horse chestnut tapped at the glass as if asking to be allowed in.

"The play you read isn't finished yet. I'll only be able to finish it together with you."

Celal lit his cigarette and motioned for him to go on. Sahir picked up his cigar, which had burnt halfway down, and neatly cut off the tip with a pair of silver scissors.

"Arif Bey was a respected man. That was obvious the first time you laid eyes on him. He had an inquisitiveness that most people were lacking. We were like old, gnarled trees, but little by little Arif stripped away the bark of our ignorance with his questions. Back at his estate in Manisa, there was never a dearth of time. Dining and prayers would end, and then he would read to us. Celal, have you ever seen frozen earth? That's what our souls were like. It's not quite ice, nor is it soil, but there are certain weeds that can take root there. From a distance they appear to be thriving, but down below they are frozen solid, useless for all practical purposes. Sure, there were certain things we took pleasure in, but everything we had was lacking in some way. It was Arif who thawed that frozen earth and brought fertility to the fields of our imagination."

Sahir got up and padded over to the window, drawing the right side of the curtain closed so that it left his face in shadow.

"Forgive me. You've come a long way and I'm sure you have questions you'd like to ask. It's been a long time since I spoke of such things. And here I find myself face to face with Arif's son… You have changed so many things in our lives. Do you know that? If you'd known, I'm sure you would have come here long ago to find me."

Celal sat up, his mind brimming with questions. "Sahir Bey, what is that play about? Why did you write it? And why did you arrange for me to find it? Who is the Police Commissioner? Who killed Jean? Who is Monsieur Pierre? And for God's sake, what is the peace machine?"

Sahir sat down in a chair facing Celal.

"Patience, dear boy. You'll get the answers to all your questions. I was born in Kudretköy. Maybe you've heard about it. According to legend, Kudretköy can be seen by the eagles that soar over the world's highest peaks. It is much more than a village. According to the locals, it is a

68

country all its own. Also according to legend, the army of Kudretköy once destroyed the surrounding villages with the hubris of might, which is fitting, since '*kudret*' itself means 'might'. When there were no more villages to conquer, the ruling families started going for each other's throats. Farriers butchered millers and shepherds slaughtered blacksmiths, and in the end the town was left in ruins. The caravans that once transported chests of treasure under the Lighthouse of Alexandria's guiding light vanished long before the lighthouse itself was destroyed.

"Why am I telling you all this? Well, Monsieur Pierre used to spend a lot of time around Kudretköy on the slopes of Mount Sipylus. If we are to believe the legends, he wouldn't have been able to do so in the town's former glory days, as the watchmen would have hauled him off to a dungeon for snooping around. But that was no longer the case. As you read in the play, I was the last of the watchman family, but I'd already run away and started working as a scribe for Arif Bey. Tahir, whose family was in charge of looking after the town's roads, occasionally saw Monsieur Pierre but didn't pay him much heed. When he first saw Monsieur Pierre, Tahir assumed he was a treasure hunter. Without thinking too much about it, he spat on the ground and started plodding in the direction of the village. At one point he came across a lizard on a stone that had recently died, probably baked to death in the heat, and out of sheer curiosity he stuck its tail in his mouth to see what it tasted like. After a few tentative nibbles he spat it out again. Within an hour he had forgotten about Monsieur Pierre and in two hours he forgot all about the lizard. The locals in nearby Manisa had at first also taken Monsieur Pierre for a treasure hunter. Unlike treasure hunters, however, he wandered around alone and was not accompanied by workers from neighbouring villages; nor did he have mules, shovels or other tools for digging. All Monsieur Pierre carried was a bag slung over his shoulder which contained some hardback books, a few changes of clothing and various magnets. He had rented an outbuilding in the yard of a home owned by a rather slovenly barrister. When his money ran out, the barrister and the other locals became firmly convinced that Pierre's buried treasure would never be found. The barrister introduced Arif Bey, who was interested in science, to Monsieur Pierre, and after that they became fast friends. That's how I first met him. Monsieur Pierre would spend a few months of the year with Arif Bey. He had a strange device that he would take up into the hills and mountains. For Arif Bey, and for me as well, Pierre was the harbinger of spring. Every year when the weather warmed up, he'd suddenly show up in a horse-drawn carriage."

Celal was quite familiar with the house in Manisa that Sahir described, the house where Arif Bey and Monsieur Pierre would spend days in discussion. Sahir also described the Red Brook where he used to go fishing, talking about it with such excitement that the water seemed to be rushing around his ankles at that very moment. Arif learnt from Sahir that there were strangely shaped electric eels that had found their way into the stream from a well in Kudretköy, and that these eels couldn't be found anywhere else.

Although the effects of the angel's trumpet Karachiyano had given him had more or less worn off by then, and Celal no longer suffered from the sudden hallucinations it had brought on, Sahir's descriptions still materialized in his mind's eye with uncanny vividness.

Pierre and Arif, arguing passionately in the courtyard of the house in Manisa…

Monsieur Pierre walking on the slopes of Mount Sipylus…

Moist-eyed Sahir as a teenager, Pierre and Arif telling him of their dream of creating a peace machine…

Monsieur Pierre trying to climb up to a cave near the peak of a mountain in the south of France and falling to his death, his body recovered only forty days later…

And then there was Céline, whose mother had died when she was giving birth. Céline, the artist, and the daughter of Monsieur Pierre…

Sahir, who ended up being put in charge of Monsieur Pierre's immense wealth, looked after Céline following her father's death.

But what interested Celal most was the peace machine.

Celal's knowledge of physics was slightly better than average, but Sahir's explanations of the theory behind the machine seemed to be magical or, more precisely, poetic rather than anything else, especially the notion of "vibrations of the soul". While he may never have fully grasped Maxwell's Equations, Celal was familiar with the fact that electricity can be transferred, even to an atom. Electrical currents are indiscriminate and have no qualms about passing between the tiniest of particles. That much made sense.

Sahir showed Celal some chapters from a medical treatise that dated back to Roman times. Scribonius Largus and Galen, both of whom were leading physicians in their day, had recommended the use of electric eels as a treatment for nervous disorders.

Sahir said, "I liked touching such eels and getting a shock. I used to lie down in the water with them in my arms. Let me tell you, young man, it certainly wasn't good for my eyes, but it helped with something else of which it would be improper of me to speak."

The knowledge had been lost over the centuries, but eventually people rediscovered that electric currents could stimulate the brain and bring on a feeling of tranquillity. In the nineteenth century, some Italian scientists had placed various metals in saltwater, effectively creating batteries, and it was said that the gentle currents they produced were good for curing fits of depression. However, no one took them very seriously at first, particularly in light of the saying "A melancholy Italian is the equivalent of a happy Frenchman."

Sahir had all the records of their experiments, and the readings they had taken of the magnetic forces around

Mount Sipylus, not to mention the results of tests made on human subjects... Drawing on all that material, Sahir had constructed a peace machine, and at last Celal had the opportunity to see the device. It consisted of a spool of copper wire, which led from a bank of batteries to numerous magnets, from which they emerged again to wind around bobbins connected to a metal ring.

"You place the metal ring on the subject's head," Sahir explained. "The electric currents suppress certain regions in the brain and stimulate others. And just as a massage for the body loosens up the joints and helps the body relax, this has a soothing effect on the brain. It doesn't last long, though—just a few days, at best creating a feeling of tranquillity that is barely perceptible. The effect is like how you feel when you drink a small shot of watered-down wine with opium. Still, it's a good start and it explains a lot. People's minds are affected by electric currents. Electromagnetic waves create certain vibrations that influence the human body, making people feel more relaxed and at peace."

Celal cut in: "May I point out that people who hang out at opium dens are relaxed and peaceful too?"

"Celal, it's not the same at all. It's possible to set up those vibrations in a way that doesn't induce lethargy. The aim of peace isn't to lead people to a life of inactivity, sprawled out on cushions on the floor, but rather to help them truly understand the universe and grasp the connection between human civilization and the essence of the universe. If it's not going to be like that, I'd even prefer war over peace. Trust me on this. My goal isn't to create an electronic opium machine. In any case, no one would bother with such a thing when we already have opium and alcohol. If I get the machine up and running, it will have to work on everyone if it is going to bring about world peace. It wouldn't be feasible to affix a metal ring to the head of every person on the planet, but there might be a way around that. Magnets draw metal towards them by invisible forces. So, by using magnets we might be able to do away with wires altogether and create a peace machine that we could set up in every city around the world. But, Celal, I won't lie to you—this isn't something that can be done today or tomorrow, but we must do our best to make great strides forward. And that is why circuses—yes, Celal, circuses—are so important!"

Just as Celal cocked an eyebrow in confusion, the knob on the living room door turned with a joyous squeak. As the door swung open, the scent of perfume filled the room, a scent like Muscat grapes that made the hair on Celal's arms rise up in salute.

Without even turning to look, Celal knew that it was Céline who had walked into the room.

6

Wild Cherries

"THAT'S SUCH BEAUTIFUL PAPER. It's handmade, isn't it? It smells almost like cherries, but a little more sour. Yes, sour cherries perhaps. The wild kind. Are sour cherries bright red or burgundy? In fact, I've never eaten a sour cherry. A Russian friend of mine told me about them once. They have them in Russia and in your country, too. How strange! Wild cherries. That's kind of an odd thing to do, insisting on eating sour cherries when we have sweet ones. I know that I'm talking through my hat when I prattle on about the wildness of sour cherries when I've never even eaten one and, in any case, I'm used to the sweet ones. I say, that sourness must leave quite a zingy feeling in your mouth. That paper is handmade, right? There's a kind of wildness about it too, and while the colour is a bit dull, it feels so nice against your fingertips.

"One night I dreamt about a cherry orchard. Sometimes when I don't know what to draw I try to fall asleep so that I'll be whisked away by dreams. That way I'll see what I should be drawing. It's really not a bad technique. But it only works if I can fall asleep."

Céline had burst into the room as quickly as she was talking. She fell silent for a moment, as if waiting for Sahir's approval to continue, and in the meantime Celal took the opportunity to stand up and face her.

Céline took him by the shoulders and gently pushed him back into the chair.

"My dear Celal, don't bother. Of course, we've been wondering about what it would be like to meet each other. Expectation dazzles the eyes and you may feel a desire to pursue whatever has stirred your desires. But you should turn a deaf ear to that urge. Eyes are for seeing and that should be enough. Just look at Sahir Bey here. He is content with his life."

Looking into Sahir's grey eyes, Celal asked, "Well, aren't you going to introduce your guests?"

A silky red handkerchief in Sahir's jacket pocket seemed to rise and daub at his moist eyelashes of its own accord.

"Celal, how much better could we get to know each other?" Céline asked. "When you wanted to know about the nape of my neck, you described the wife of an Italian composer at the palace in complete detail, with one exception: her neck. The same would go for the arse of that Ethiopian woman, which you sketched in the briefest of terms. To be honest, the way you played that little game of yours made me feel as if someone was spying on me through a hole in the wall, waiting for me to pull up my skirt.

"It's like sleep. You know, sometimes sleep is a steep slope. If you're at the top, it's easy, like gliding down a slide. If I can't sleep, how am I supposed to dream, and how am I supposed to see what I'm supposed to draw? I also imagine caves. A cave filled with countless bats hanging upside down. I close my eyes. The bats squeak and my voice becomes one with theirs. I sprout wings and my back itches a little but then the steep slope angles down… And there you have it, I'm asleep."

Sahir was standing there, still holding the handkerchief to his eyes. For a moment Celal was unable to summon the courage to look back at Céline.

He said, "Well, it sounds like a lot of work. After all that, you deserve to have the most fascinating of dreams."

"Celal, would you believe it? I've never actually dreamt, not once. I lied because I envy people who dream. I've never dreamt of a cherry orchard. But I'd rather believe that I had and had then forgotten about it. I never dream. Jean once told me the silliest thing I ever heard—he said that I don't dream because my ancestors were Atlantean. As you may know, Herodotus wrote about the history of the people of Atlantis. One of the most interesting things he said was that they never dreamt. You see, so it is possible that I'm half Atlantean. Jean was always coming up with such wild ideas. If my ancestors were from Atlantis, they had probably got their fill of revelry and settled in a quiet French village. I mean, my ancestors on my mother's side. I'm willing to bet that being an Atlantean can only be passed down by mothers. My father wasn't from the village. He was a city man, and a professor, too. A professor of physics, and geology, and chemistry. If you ask me, I think he dabbled in alchemy. I'm sure that he dreamt. If you don't dream, why would you throw yourself into solving the mysteries of the universe?"

As Celal listened to her, he realized that Céline was not just beautiful—she was stunning. She had deep-blue eyes that caught your gaze and refused to let go. Her cheeks had a pinkness typical of the villagers on her mother's side, and they tapered to a slightly pointed chin. Thick blonde curls framed her slender neck, resting on her shoulders.

Celal's dream illustrator, now finally standing before him in the flesh, was wearing a black dress in the Native American style that was embroidered with red stripes from the collar to the hem. As she stood there looking at Celal, she was thumping a tomahawk into her palm. Celal found it difficult to think of anything to say at first. At last he managed, "Indeed, that is handmade paper. I went to great lengths to have it shipped from abroad. A lot of people think that our art is lacking in morals, that it is crude and coarse. But there's an excitement to doing crude work of the highest calibre. I am of the belief that a true aesthetic consists of the right balance of coarseness and pleasure."

Céline stopped swinging the tomahawk. Celal took a step towards her and said, "I think that your drawings, which provide the greatest of pleasure, are perfect in that regard. *Primo*, people always opt for pleasurable coarseness over coarse pleasures. *Secundo*, your troubles with sleep are of no great interest to me. That is to say, at least right now. *Tertio*, and most important, is the matter of Jean's death. How did you know him? But before broaching those issues, common sense dictates that I first ask you: why are you dressed up like a native of the Americas?"

"A true Ottoman Sherlock Holmes… Is that what you think you are? Methodological, and wild like cherries, yet endowed with the cunning of a man from the East. I couldn't have come up with a more clichéd, commonplace character."

"Well, madame, I'd say that's no worse than being dressed up like a Native American in a luxurious apartment in Paris. That, I'd say, is the ultimate commonplace."

"Ha, that's precisely the Oriental slyness I was talking about. Celal, do you know what ordinariness is? A reality that has lost its vivacity, novelty and ability to surprise, in the end becoming a mere formula. Perhaps a little like a still life, don't you think? The outfit I'm wearing is for a modern still life. Sahir enjoys photography and he likes to take photographs of his dearest friends in, let's say, novel ways. Sahir, isn't that true?"

Sahir was gazing out of the window, his attention elsewhere. He got up and closed the curtains, plunging the living room into darkness.

Celal turned to Sahir.

"Sir, listening to this lady's sweet chatter some other time would give me more pleasure that you can imagine. After all, I have always been a great admirer of the illustrations in my books. I would be lying if I said that I hadn't imagined coming to Paris and meeting her. Normally, I am a man who has much time to spare. However, now I have pressing matters to which I must attend. I'm sure you are quite aware that the play you wrote and the story you told me have aroused my interest very much indeed, and I would like to thank you for your hospitality. But if I'm not offered a convincing explanation for why I've been led here, our last communication will consist of the thanks I have extended to you."

Sahir silently tucked his handkerchief back into his pocket and furrowed his brow. Celal started heading down the hall towards the front door, and as he passed by Céline he took a deep breath, filling his lungs with the scent of Muscat grapes. As he turned the doorknob, Sahir said, "My dear Celal, are you fond of circuses?"

Celal paused.

Sahir approached him and said, "Come now, you can't really dislike circuses," offering Celal a clown-like grin that stretched from ear to ear.

"Going to the circus is one thing, but being in one is quite another. Celal, I was in fact making you a job offer. I do believe that being part of a circus that is dedicated to a lofty cause will be good for everyone involved. Of course, you are free to go, but please hear me out first."

"On one condition."

Céline called out from the living room, "And what condition might that be?"

"Tell me what happened to Jean."

Sahir guided Celal back to the living room.

"I promise I'll tell you everything I know. Jean loved the circus, and I'm sure that you will too."

Céline threw a pink shawl of twisted silk over her bare shoulders and stretched out on the carpet, propping her head up with one hand. Celal sat down on one of the dining chairs.

"Did Jean work for the circus?"

Sahir sighed. "No, he was working for me. You must work hard if you want to bring peace into the world. We've been trying to do business as far afield as we can. Please don't think that I'm exaggerating when I say this, but Jean was involved in what I could call the shadier side of our business. The side where even the slightest altercation can have far-reaching consequences. I've been searching high and low for clues about what happened to him. I hope that I will soon come upon a satisfactory answer. I won't lie to you—my relationship with Jean had soured recently. That's why the police suspect that I had something to do with his disappearance. I need to find his murderer as soon as possible, so that I can get the police off my back. If you can give me a little time, I'll return the money that was stolen from you."

Celal shook his head. "It seems to me that Jean's murder is far from being a simple matter. The police don't seem to suspect you. After all, I was the one who was taken into custody so that your play could be passed on to me by none other than the Police Commissioner, who, it seems, is in your pocket."

"It's the same in every country. If you have clout, if need be you can always find someone to grease the wheels or throw a spanner in the works. The Commissioner is one of those people. For the time being he is keeping me out of the investigation. I guessed that you would come to France when you heard about Jean's death, so I asked the Commissioner to keep an eye on the passenger records at the port. But you had set off before Jean was killed. Of course, I arranged for the Commissioner to give you that notebook. I must confess, I wanted to surprise you and make sure that you were intrigued. Please forgive me. Eventually this business is going to come back to me. That's why I have to work out what happened before the police do. Jean was quite the maverick, and he probably thought it would be humiliating to come to me for help. Please believe me, Celal, when I tell you that Jean and Céline are precious to me, and I owe it to Pierre to look after them. I won't have any peace of mind until I solve this mystery."

Céline said, "None of us will have any peace of mind. But it's almost morning, and I'm starving. Can we please have something to eat?"

There was a button at the end of the table. Sahir reached over and pressed it twice, and there was a faint ringing in the back of the apartment. A few moments later a butler appeared, set a covered tray on the table, and then disappeared as quickly as he'd come. Sahir, Celal and Céline ate breakfast in silence.

Celal said, "I'm going to try to trust you, Sahir Bey. If I were in your position, I'd make sure I kept my word. Please don't disappoint me or the memory of Jean."

Sahir had given Celal a fake passport, identity card and military papers. Celal stacked them up as he sat at the table, running his fingers over the pages in silence. After drumming his fingers on the table for a while, he smiled and pretended to introduce himself: "Petar Jovanovic, how do you do?… The name's Petar Jovanovic…"

He tied up the stack of papers with a thick piece of string. Weighing the bundle in his hand, he turned to Sahir and said, "As if that whole business of being Şerif Efendi wasn't enough… Now I'm supposed to be Petar Jovanovic! Would it have overtaxed your imagination to come up with a more interesting name than that?"

"Well, my boy, in addition to playing the part of Petar Jovanovic, an officer in the Serbian army, you will also be playing the role of the Colossus, our circus's animal-skin-clad strongman. What more could you want?"

"Very well, being the Colossus will be easy. I've been surprising people with feats of strength since I was a child.

But being an officer? Especially with a name like that... It grates on the ears."

"If I were you, I'd be more worried about the circus act. Going on stage is anything but easy. In the end, acting isn't just a matter of pretending to be someone else, and being in a circus act is pure acting."

"Yes, but I'm going to be putting on an act to play the role of Petar Jovanovic, too."

"Sure, but aside from two of our contacts no one will know that you're playing a role, so you'll feel more at ease than any stage actor has ever felt—precisely because you won't be taking to the stage. What makes actors unique is that they can play a role fully aware of the fact that the audience knows that they're acting. Nearly everyone could act if no one knew that they were acting, just like everyone can sing when there's no audience."

"That's all very well, but I'll have to speak Serbian, since I'm going to be in the Serbian army."

"Celal, you're a child of the Balkans. You can already speak Serbian and you have a knack for languages. Jean told me that you were translating some books of Serbian fairy tales just to pass the time. Just make sure you roll your 'r's like a Frenchman. It'll make things easier."

"Why?"

"You're going to turn up quite suddenly, so we've created a past for you. You'll have to be convincing enough that people will come to trust you, and mysterious enough to inspire a little admiration. So, listen carefully. You, Petar Jovanovic, are not really from Serbia. You're from a family of Bosnian Serbs. That'll make it easier for you to get on with the more radical officers in the army. They're all obsessed with saving the Serbs who have been taken captive by the Habsburgs. Your father went to France to study history and married a Frenchwoman there. He taught history at a high school, and died at a young age. You joined the military academy so that you wouldn't be a burden on your mother. As you've seen, all your documents testify to that story. You know that some people in the government wield great influence. If anyone doubts the authenticity of your papers and questions anyone at the consulate or even the municipality in Paris, people in the highest ranks will say that your papers are real."

Celal sat back in his chair and asked, "Am I going to pretend to be half French because it was easier to get the papers sorted out here?"

"Partly. And if you get in trouble, you speak French like it's your native language, which will make your story all the more convincing. But the real reason is Karageorgevic. He's the head of the dynasty competing with Obrenovic, the Serbian king. He, too, graduated from the French military academy. If anyone asks, tell them that you've never had the honour of meeting him. But we're quietly going to put out word among our men that you're working for Karageorgevic."

"That's a great tactic if your goal is to get me executed."

"Sarcasm will certainly come in handy when you're playing the part of Petar Jovanovic. Our men will relish the thought that you're working for the Karageorgevic dynasty in one way or another. Certain elements in the army are plotting a coup. They want to take down Obrenovic and put Karageorgevic in power. But they have doubts about whether or not Karageorgevic will go along with the plan. The poor guy is too genteel for that kind of excitement. Also, they're in dire need of help from France. If they don't get the French on their side against the Habsburgs, their revolution will most certainly be short-lived. Your presence there will be seen as a sign that Karageorgevic and the French are in favour of the coup. So please, don't worry about your safety. We've already taken measures to ensure that no harm will come to you."

"Sahir Bey?"

"What is it, Celal?"

"I'd like you to be open with me."

"I've been as open with you as I possibly can."

"Why am I going to Serbia to help spark a revolution with a group of people I've only just heard about? If you ask me, this all seems more like a shadowy plot than a struggle for peace."

"So you're happy to be the Colossus at the circus, but the part about Serbia concerns you, is that right?"

"At least working at the circus sounds somewhat entertaining."

"I'm not sure which is going to be more entertaining. But at the very least, stirring up coups lends itself more to improvisation. The business of revolutions is all about experimentation and drills. Celal, every country in the world, and I mean every single country, is being dragged to the brink of war. If we don't stop it, a major war is going to break out in ten, maybe fifteen years. It'll be a war unlike any other. The world is a smaller place than it's ever been before. Now you can go to places in a week or two that used to take months to reach. And the same holds true for armies. There's a very good chance that if war does break out, it will engulf the entire world. We're no longer living in the age of Alexander the Great, Caesar, Genghis Khan or Suleiman the Magnificent. If a war breaks out, there's no power out there that can come along with an 'I say, what seems to be the problem here?' and bring it to an end. Such a war would be more terrifying than we can imagine.

"Now, Karageorgevic doesn't have his eye on the Serbian throne, but if the revolutionaries promise to hand power to a new parliament, along with a new constitution that guarantees freedom for everyone, he will go along with their plan. Be assured, Celal, his aim is to be the last Serbian king and pass his power over to the people through a parliament. But with or without Karageorgevic, the plotters will go ahead with their coup. They're champing at the bit, waiting for a chance to bring down the old monarchy. And if we help them to succeed in Serbia, the other kingdoms of Europe will soon fall in turn. If we don't bring those kingdoms down now, they will ultimately perish in a world war. But if the people take power in one country after another... everywhere, from London to Istanbul... that will be the first step towards eternal peace. And if we can build the peace machine when the time is right—"

Celal cut him off: "If that peace machine you've been going on about is truly so wondrous, wouldn't the same results be achieved if it were used on all the world's kings, sultans and generals?"

Sahir blinked and then sighed, placing his hand on Celal's shoulder. "Electromagnetism," he said, "is perhaps the most democratic force in the world. It exists everywhere in every single moment. It has the power to influence every single person's soul. You're right. If we could use the machine on those people who make decisions about war and peace, our work would be much easier.

"But we have Monsieur Pierre's calculations. It could work for one, maybe two generations. Another problem, however, is that we don't have a power source that is strong enough to make the machine work. We're just not ready. And what's more, the human race is so complex—there are some people whose souls will never respond to it. The entire project could be shattered by just one king or sultan who is not affected by the peace machine, because they could drive their peace-loving citizens to war. True, we hold the key to world peace. But if it were to be used in the wrong way, the already warped order that humanity has brought into being would be destroyed. Celal, that's why the people should rule their countries. We will activate the machine when every single country is freed from the aggression of its ruler. And then no one will think of going to war, howl battle cries or hack at people's throats with daggers. No, Celal, using the peace machine to take down only kings, queens, sultans, maharajas or tsars simply would not do. The democracy of electromagnetism requires that countries themselves be democratic.

"Arif once said to me, 'People do not want to go to war unless they're driven to fight.' Meaning that, if people were left to decide for themselves whether or not to go to war, the chance of war breaking out would be slight. But as well as giving power to the people, we need something that can soothe their troubled souls. Pierre discovered that something, or at least he discovered the *way* to that something. You know, Celal, all across the world there are immense war machines designed for the sole purpose of killing. A thousand years ago, who could have imagined that ships of iron could float? Who would have ever believed that a piece of metal no bigger than your little finger could be fired from a metal contraption that fits in your hand, and kill an enemy far, far away? Well, we will build a peace machine to oppose their war machines, and once our machine has done its work on people's minds and souls, nobody will ever think of war again. But first of all, the people must have a say in government so that the peace machine can offer a remedy for their woes."

The Orient Express departed from Paris, making its way to Strasbourg and from there to Munich. It would have been conspicuous if Celal and Céline had travelled together in a private compartment, so they stayed in separate cars. During the two weeks they'd spent in Paris and throughout the train journey, Celal had been making subtle romantic overtures to Céline which she had brushed aside, sometimes graciously and sometimes with far less tact. Still, as the train steamed towards Vienna, Celal found himself praying that it would break down so that he could spend more time with Céline. The train, however, appeared to have no intention of breaking down. As it rolled steadily along the tracks, Celal silently cursed the engineers who had designed the sturdy 2-4-0-class locomotive and decided that he would try to enjoy his dinner with Céline in the dining car as best he could.

"I've realized that I really like travelling by train. The fact that the earth is round has always frightened me. I worry that the people on the bottom half of the earth will fall off. It's not just the people, though: mountains, build-ings, trees, oceans… I'm scared by the idea that everything will be gone. No, that's not it… It's more like I worry that it's not quite clear what is on the top and what is on the bottom. After all, the earth is just a ball in a void. Maybe we're the ones on the bottom. For me, the idea that I'm hanging upside down is completely unacceptable, even humiliating! I'm sure you've heard that most people dream of falling. As for me, I feel like I'm falling when I'm awake. But that strange feeling vanishes when I'm travelling by train. The rails are secured firmly to the earth and the train glides along them as if the earth is perfectly flat. It's like the way that having a ceiling above your head reassures you that you're not going to fly off into nothingness."

Céline settled deep into the leather seat in the Wagons-Lits dining car and held out her crystal wine glass to Celal: "Cheers." Smacking her lips, she went on. "I've realized how fond I am of oysters, wild duck, charcuterie boards and mixed dessert platters. True, Sahir has never been stingy, but this time he really has shown no mercy to his money. Then again, you never know—he might even own this train. Sometimes it shocks me to realize that a person I know well is actually something of a mystery to me."

"Do you trust Sahir?"

"I place my trust in my father, not Sahir. You see, I simply can't accept that he dedicated his life to a fantasy, that he died on some far-off mountain all for the sake of a fantasy. Actually that's just the official line. Truth be told, I understand nothing of electromagnetism, or of how the peace machine works. To be honest, my dear Celal, the real reason that I got involved in all this was for the fun of it. Have you noticed that I'm a little superficial? I struggled for a long time with that. In the end, I lost the struggle. That's just how I am. I'm not interested in much aside from travelling the world and working on my pictures, and the circus is a great way to explore the world. I've been to so many countries and seen so many cities. And it makes me happy to think that if one day I have grandchildren, they will brag to their friends that their grandma was once a lion tamer."

Celal picked up the chicken leg on his plate and took a savage bite out of it.

"I stole a chicken when I was a boy."

"Just one?"

"And some goats."

"Your grandchildren probably aren't going to brag about you as much as mine will about me."

"What, do you think being the Colossus at the circus is going to be child's play?"

"Not exactly. But a lion tamer? Clearly nothing beats that. And it requires great expertise."

"Let me ask you this: do you think you'll acquire that expertise by the time we get to Belgrade?"

"I'll get off in Vienna, where I'll join the circus. We have some shows there, so I'll have time to work on my routine. Then we have shows scheduled in most of the other Habsburg cities, too. There's little chance of a revolution breaking out there, but being in a circus is a great way to gather intelligence and sow the seeds of revolution. We'll spend about six months touring in Austria-Hungary before we go to Serbia. That'll give you enough time to work your way into the ranks of the revolutionaries in Belgrade. Just make sure you don't kill anyone along the way."

"So when will I see you again?"

Céline picked up her knife and, looking into Celal's eyes, took his right hand. A slight smile tugged at her lips before she dragged the knife across his palm, making a deep cut. Then she picked up a napkin from the table and pressed it on the smile-shaped wound.

"We will see each other again before this has healed."

She took a piece of paper out of her purse.

"Sahir thinks that this young lieutenant may make things easier for you. His name is Dragan Petrovic. They'll tell you in Belgrade where to find him."

Céline got up and started heading for the door of the dining car.

"Céline!"

She stopped and turned around.

"What happened to Jean? Why was he killed?"

"Celal, please. That's another story. You'll find everything out when the time is right."

Céline turned back towards the door, which Celal rushed to hold open for her. As she gave him a nod of thanks, he placed his bloodied hand on the back of her neck and kissed her lightly on the lips.

"We will meet again before you have forgotten about that kiss," he said.

Céline laughed. "Celal, I don't think your grandchildren will brag about what you just did."

"Until we meet again."

7

The Young Lieutenant

D RAGAN PETROVIC spent much of the spring of 1903 consumed by dreams of marriage. But because he had done the same in the winter months of 1901 and the summer months of 1902, no one took him very seriously.

Those winter months had been bitterly cold yet Dragan Petrovic's heart was aflame with the desire to marry Maria, his landlord's spinster daughter. Maria's hips were of such voluptuous girth that she was unable to pass through the narrow doorways of most of the old shops in Belgrade. The doorways of the shops in the newer buildings, built in the Viennese style, could accommodate her hips, but those were quite beyond her means.

So that's how everything started between them: lanky Dragan, a young lieutenant, started going shopping for Maria. There wasn't a single doorway that he couldn't pass through.

In that chilly winter of 1901, Maria's curves filled Dragan with a warmth that seeped into the depths of his being. With his black eyebrows and red moustache, the lieutenant would set off in the evening, stomping through the frozen mud in search of lace, slips, socks, shoes and hats, dreaming of how one day he would strip them from Maria's body.

Then, as the weather began warming up, Maria's hips started to become an obsession for Dragan, like a fishbone stuck in his throat.

He had dreamt of a home with the broadest of doorways, a home where he and Maria would spend the long winter months together. And then that dream was wrenched from his hands.

Towards the middle of spring he found out that he was being transferred to Deligrad, a town in the east. The fishbone started to work its way loose, and when he moved out with his few possessions he became nothing more than a former tenant to Maria, just one of the five young men who had helped her with her shopping.

Maria had never had the slightest interest in Dragan. Young moustachioed men of slender build simply didn't set her heart racing. No, she longed for a man with a thick black beard and flashing eyes, a man of few words. And when her heart pounded, the sound could be heard two streets away. It wasn't because of her broad hips that she'd never got married. Rather, she'd just never met anyone crazy-hearted enough to be able to handle her.

Never knowing that Maria had referred to him as "that toothpick boy", Dragan set off wracked by pangs of remorse, but at the same time he was filled with an equally powerful feeling of relief. In addition, the prospect of spending the summer in Deligrad appealed to him. Everyone knew they had fought two great battles against the Turks there, but knowing that is one thing and breathing in the scent of blood and gunpowder as a patriotic young soldier wearing a uniform drenched in sweat is quite another. Wandering the battlefield daydreaming about how Karayorgo had driven off Ibrahim Pasha and the Janissaries made his spirits soar to lofty heights and set his heart pounding with zeal.

In the town square of Deligrad there was an old villager who would sing a song about the legend of Milos Obilic, the hero who'd killed the sultan with a blow of his dagger:

"Obilic, son of the Dragon / Took wing for the plain / He drew his dagger / And stabbed the Sultan straight in the heart…"

Dejana, the villager's granddaughter, had hair that reached down to her waist. As her grandfather's voice breathed sweet pain into Dragan's soul, the curls of her hair worked their way into his heart. For Dragan, Dejana glowed like the new sun of the old Kingdom of Serbia. Although she was rather petite, when she sang along with her grandfather she looked as though she could cleave the Plain of Deligrad in two with a sword and rend asunder the chains of Serbian captives with smouldering coals plucked from deep in the earth.

Dragan's moustache stood tall and proud, and his spine seemed to have taken on the hardness of a diamond. He had it all worked out. He was going to set up a home with Dejana, a simple place befitting their homeland. He'd already decided that he was going to ask the old man for his grand-daughter's hand in marriage.

However, when summer gave way to autumn, Dejana's hair quickly lost its lustre. The curls hanging to her waist became matted and tangled like dead moss. As autumn settled in, Dragan's misery grew deeper as the shadows grew longer. His admiration for Dejana waned day by day, making him feel as though he'd betrayed his people. In the midst of that depression, he once thought of committing suicide with his ceremonial sword on the Plain of Deligrad so that his blood would seep into the soil, absolving him of his sin.

But he would never remember that thought later, because it occurred to him one night just seconds before he passed out on his hard bed after drinking a copious amount of wine, a boot dangling from his foot.

What saved Dragan Petrovic from the shame of his expired love was an unexpected summons to Belgrade.

It was the middle of winter in 1903. In order to avoid running across broad-hipped Maria, he rented a flat in an attic on Skadar Street, which was far from his old neighbourhood. Nearly everyone else living in the four-storey building worked in the palace kitchens.

In truth, it wouldn't normally have been possible for him to rent a place on Skadar Street on his salary, but a captain he'd met in Deligrad, one Petar Jovanovic, had said that the landlord was a friend of his and would give him a good deal.

So Dragan Petrovic moved in, paying a third of the usual rent. He would never find out that Celal was paying the rest, or that the owner of the building ran a press that printed political flyers of the most radical kind.

With the help of an officer he met through Sahir, Celal had located lieutenant Petrovic in Deligrad. He'd found him standing in the town square listening misty-eyed to an old man sing songs of heroism. By pulling some strings, Celal had had Dragan Petrovic reassigned to Belgrade.

Towards the end of winter, Dragan met Apis. He also fell in love with Vesna Jevric, a young woman who worked at the palace, and yet again the longing to marry stirred in his heart.

At around three o'clock one Saturday afternoon, Dragan met up with Celal. Both men were wearing civilian clothes, as Celal had planned. Celal led Dragan down an alley that led from the rather ritzy Zeleni Venac Square, walking slowly at first and then quickening his steps until he stopped in front of a building. He looked around to make sure that no one was watching, and motioned for Dragan to follow him as he started making his way down a narrow flight of stairs.

At the bottom of the stairs there was a rusty-green steel door, invisible from the street, above which was a sign that read "The Acorn". Dragan had heard about the place. It was a tavern where revolutionaries and officers were rumoured to gather along with the most radical representatives of the National Assembly, which the King would dissolve whenever it suited his whim. According to some, revelries were held there with women of dubious morals.

Radovan, his neighbour in the building on Skadar Street and the palace's head pastry chef, had told Dragan about one such night as if he had been there himself. He caught hold of Dragan's arm in the narrow stairwell where they were talking and whispered unspeakable things in his ear. Naturally, Dragan responded frostily. "I forbid you from speaking to me of such matters," he said, trying to defend the honour of his uniform and the army.

All the same, in his dreams he began to see revolutionaries in gleaming helmets as they sat atop powerful horses, the grateful faces of their rescued comrades gazing up at them. Then the scene would shift and he'd find himself passionately making love to a woman in a high-ceilinged room with marble floors, a place he'd realize was The Acorn.

One morning he woke from such dreams, and as he was walking out of the house Radovan greeted him with a lecher's conspiratorial wink. Dragan felt quite uneasy at moments like that. He would even think about going to the bathhouse run by a Bosnian from Novi Pazar in an attempt to cleanse himself. But the thought of the bathhouse just made him feel all the more guilty, so he prayed and prayed, trying to find peace of mind.

Celal rapped on the steel door three times and it swung open, filling the narrow stairwell with the sound of men's voices, thick tobacco smoke and the sour smell of alcohol.

Even though the stench of debauchery made his stomach turn, Dragan followed Celal inside. This unexpected turn of events rattled Dragan, making his bladder and intestines suddenly convulse with painful cramps.

Inside the tavern, everyone was listening with rapt attention to a man giving an impassioned speech. The speaker was wearing nondescript clothes and was completely bald, except for a woolly tuft of dark hair above each of his ears. He had a bulbous nose like that of a ventriloquist's puppet, thick lips, an unremarkable forehead, and a rather Teutonic moustache. His hairless pate was covered in splotches of sweat, a trickle of which was running down his left temple.

Unable to contain himself, Dragan asked Celal, "Is that Dragutin Dimitrijevic?"

Celal nodded and with the faintest of smiles said, "Now be quiet, young lieutenant, and listen to what Apis has to say."

Apis's voice was not impressive, and his words were not particularly moving. His attire, expressions and appearance all came across as quite ordinary. But somehow all of that ordinariness so decisively combined in a single person was in itself striking, magically transforming Apis into a demigod in the eyes of his admirers.

The fifty or so tough-looking men in the café were as tame as kittens as they listened to the speech, silent apart from the occasional murmur of approval.

"That soft-bellied Alexander Obrenovic took over the kingdom and now he's shaking his arse in front of two whores, just biding his time before he rapes the people's freedom. The first of those whores is that dotard Franz Joseph in Vienna, the depraved head of the Habsburg dynasty which hides its incestuous, twisted face behind bushy sideburns. He is the gaoler of the prison where they keep our people, a trader in our captive comrades."

With the slender fingers of his right hand Apis wiped away the sweat on his forehead and shook it off on the floor.

"The second whore is Queen Draga."

He spat after saying her name, and everyone else in the café followed suit. In a matter of seconds the floor was covered in a layer of spit hacked up from lungs filled with tobacco-brown phlegm. Not wanting to attract attention, Dragan was going to spit as well; but afraid that the spittle would stick to his moustache, which he had so meticulously groomed that morning, he made do with pretending. Celal noticed Dragan's ruse and smiled.

"The vile progeny of a drunkard mother and lunatic father... Her Czech husband's sloppy seconds. She's handled cocks you wouldn't even touch with a blind beggar's walking stick. That whore has slept with more men than the sluttiest of whores you've ever screwed. And Alexander, who took over as head of the Serbs as king, is a pup led around on the leash of that alleyway tramp, rolling around on the ground hoping for a belly rub."

Some of the men swore and banged their pewter beer mugs on the wooden tables.

"I say 'pup' because we've seen what his father was like. Didn't King Milan offer up Belgrade on a golden platter to those monkey-bearded Habsburg bastards? And why didn't Vienna swoop down on us when he bowed and scraped before them? Fear. Because they were afraid that we'd rise up. They were afraid that our comrades taken captive by the Habsburgs would revolt. But you see, Milan would have been happy to sell us out if he could have. And while Alexander is just a pup compared to Milan when it comes to being a spineless coward, even Milan didn't go so far as to insult the Serbs by marrying a slut."

Standing near the bar, a barrel-chested man with a thick grey moustache drunkenly shouted, "And a barren slut at that!"

Apis was taken aback by the interruption, especially since he had just reached his speech's most titillating point, but since the man had raised a subject that he was going to discuss anyway he went on: "She's barren and she's a liar. Didn't they announce that she was pregnant last year? And then what happened? Did she have a miscarriage? No! She was never pregnant. It was a lie! All the European newspapers mock this lying whore of a Serbian queen. Schoolchildren run around chanting, 'They have a queen who is a whore, and Serbia is the whore of the Habsburgs!' Since he can't have his own children, Alexander named that slut queen's brother his heir. When Alexander dies, is Nikola, the drunkard brother of a whore, going to be king? Is Nikola, who once killed a poor police officer just for fun while out on a drinking spree, going to be the saviour of the Serbs?"

Apis had reached the end of his speech, but the crowd didn't respond with applause or enthusiasm. Instead, silent anger filled the café, thicker than the smoke hanging in the air.

After finishing his drink, the orator got up and walked towards a door behind the bar that Dragan hadn't noticed before, followed by three other men. Apis shot Celal a stern look and hissed, "Jovanovic," motioning for Celal and Dragan to join him.

Unable to bear the pressure in his bladder and intestines, however, Dragan, whose face was beetroot-red by this point, quickly shuffled off in the direction of the lavatory.

8

A Fool's Aid

D RAGAN PETROVIC was lying on the ground in an emerald-green meadow, the branch of a lilac tree blooming with purple flowers brushing against his forehead. Translucent smoke from a giant censer slowly snaked into his nostrils, but he didn't sneeze. Quite on the contrary, he felt more and more at ease. He could feel his muscles relaxing, and he closed his eyes.

As he stretched out his arms and legs, he realized that he was actually floating on water. The earth and scented flowers had given way to ripples that smelt of iodine. There was a finely woven sheet covering the lieutenant, and lilac petals gently rained down on its surface.

When he slowly opened his long-lashed eyes, he saw beams of light among the petals drifting down over him. To his right and left, little swirls and eddies pulled the petals on the water's dappled surface down into the depths.

He was surprised to see that the sheet wasn't getting wet. It had merely become transparent and was still covering him, leaving only the tip of his nose and his eyes exposed.

The petals carried by the little eddies slowly flowed down the stream and filled the lake. Everything was covered in lilac petals.

Dragan then found himself immersed in a stream of lilac petals. The smoke pouring from the censer was getting thicker, filling the air, blanketing everything.

His muscles, already relaxed, went completely limp. The young lieutenant, Serbia's great hope, was lying beneath a sheet made of lilac petals. He could hear a song being sung, ever so faintly. He wondered if it could be Dejana from Deligrad, Dejana whose hair hung to her waist.

As he tried to picture her lips, he felt a sudden jab in his head and metal grating against his skull. The sound echoed in his head, turning into that song, filling all the empty spaces of his mind.

The pain that started at the top of his head spread over his body like a net, each and every filament cutting into his skin. He felt like he was being cut to pieces and that he would bleed out under the lilac petals, never to be seen again.

First he forgot the song, note by note, and then his name, letter by letter. Then he forgot that he'd forgotten his name. All the same, he knew that something was wrong. The smoke was getting thicker and the pain was so intense that it paralysed his mind, but eventually he forgot everything, even that he existed. He became nothingness, non-existence.

Nothingness Dragan.

Lost Dragan.

Non-existent Dragan.

Let go, Dragan. Give in.

"Dragan! Dragan! Dragan Petrovic, wake up! That's an order!"

Celal's booming voice drove everything from his thoughts except the lilac petals, and the dream faded out.

Dragan was in such pain that he couldn't open his eyes, but when Celal saw him shift ever so slightly under the sheet and utter a weak moan he knew that the lieutenant was awake.

The attic flat on Skadar Street may have been fairly new, but it had already witnessed its own fair share of strange scenes.

There had been the medical student, who had sliced open his wrists with surgical precision from a sense of melancholy that even he himself didn't understand.

There had been the two young civil servants who stabbed each other to death, out of fear of what would happen to them if it was discovered that they made love.

There had been the ageing bachelor, who died after accidentally inhaling poisonous fumes while burning love letters from his fiancée of many years.

There had been that bizarre husband and wife, who had moved in with a goat that they milked in the living room. The man was so fond of milking the goat that when it died he cut off its teats and had them stuffed. The couple moved out, unable to bear the loss of the goat, the man carrying the stuffed teats under one arm and his wife holding on to the other.

Dragan was the latest link in that long chain of tenants, but he wasn't the strangest person the attic flat had welcomed through its door.

If it had been just a commonplace apartment, not such a worldly-wise one, and witnessed the scene of Celal in all the glory of his military uniform standing over that frail, long-faced man covered in bandages as he lay on the thin mattress of that wooden bed, then surely it would have shuddered at the sight, down to its very beams and posts.

Dragan's bed was in the living room along with the rest of his meagre furniture: a low wooden table, two chairs and a small wardrobe.

Celal leant down and blew hard on the lieutenant's face. When Dragan opened his eyes, Celal stepped back.

"It all happened in six minutes, Petrovic. I know, because I checked my watch when Apis and I went in, and I kept my eye on it all the while. No one pays enough attention to things like that, but if you're going to have discipline you have to always keep track of time. I even sent the military academy a few petitions, asking them to add a class about horology. That way, restless officer candidates would learn the meaning of patience, and when they get kicked out of the academy they'll have a vocation."

Dragan tried to sit up. The pain in his chest, which was wrapped tightly in bandages, brought tears to his eyes but he managed to prop himself up so that he could turn towards Celal.

"Let me give you an example, Petrovic. If you had taken a course in horology at the academy, *primo*, you wouldn't have gone off and so openly asked where Apis was holding the meeting about the coup, thereby bringing upon yourself the most well-deserved beating of your life. *Secundo*, when you get kicked out of the military for your idiocy, you'd have a job. I know what they say: 'Jovanovic is always sending rather eccentric petitions to his superiors, which is why he's still a captain while his former classmates are all colonels.' But the thing is, I've thought it all through and my requests are always based on experience. *Tertio*, I'm always right, in a way that even you can understand. You've got long, delicate fingers. If the commander at the military academy had actually logged my petitions, by next week you'd be set up as an horologist in a small town somewhere."

It took a while for Dragan to make any sense of what he was hearing. Celal was standing over him menacingly, uttering each word with such firm conviction that his sword swung from his hip like the pendulum of a cuckoo clock.

Dragan chewed his lower lip, trying to remember what had happened. Based on the bandages and pain he was in, he knew that something was amiss.

The last thing the young lieutenant remembered was going to the lavatory at The Acorn. He surmised that he must have done something foolish and then got a thrashing at the hands of Apis's men, the shame of which he could readily accept. Being kicked out of the army and subjected to the stinging words of this commander, however, was too much for him to bear.

Dragan wanted to run away and hide but he knew that it was pointless, so he closed his eyes and tried to whisk himself back to the emerald-green meadow of his dream, whereupon he received a resounding slap to the face. Two large hands grabbed him by the shoulders and propped him against the wall by the bed. His broken ribs dug into his flesh but the sudden movement seemed to knock his lungs and brain back into place. Celal's surly strength was not the kind to trifle with.

"Exactly six minutes, Petrovic. Six minutes. That's how long you were in the lavatory. Who knows what the hell you were thinking, but in the end they beat you unconscious. Why? For saying that a secret society was going to restore the glory of the country by overthrowing the King and Queen and saving our comrades from captivity. For mentioning the members of the society by name. And you managed to do all that in six minutes. Bravo. That's quite a feat."

Dragan opened his mouth to reply but Celal was like a charging locomotive gathering speed, determined to thunder on even if it meant flying off the tracks. Angrily he pulled his sword halfway out of its scabbard and slammed it back in with a clatter, which was enough to make the pale-faced lieutenant close his mouth. As Celal stood there, anchored in place by rage, the sword went on swinging at his side.

But then something happened which caught Dragan off guard. The captain started laughing. At first it was a titter like the cooing of a dove, the sound spreading out like ripples on a pond. But as Celal opened his mouth wider and his body started to tremble, the cooing changed. The walls of the small apartment echoed with the sound of his laughter, which by now was like the squawking of seagulls, and Dragan's eyes widened as the echo roared in his ears.

The young lieutenant, having awoken from a dream only to find himself in a nightmare, realized as he watched Celal that if he didn't speak then, he would never speak again. "Captain," he managed to mutter, "I beg of you…"

Those words managed to stem the crescendo of Celal's laughter, which was still resonating through the flat. Celal looked at him, a demented smile twisting his lips.

His head already throbbing, Dragan could bear it no longer. "Captain," he said, "I don't remember what happened yesterday but it must have been an unpardonable mistake. Please let me resign and, if possible, restore my honour. I always wanted to die on the battlefield, taken down by a bullet. So give the order. I will resign and save myself from this shame with a single shot from my gun." Celal fell silent. After a moment he walked over to one of the chairs and, grabbing it with one hand, dragged it over to the bed and slowly sat down.

"It wasn't yesterday," Celal said. "You've been unconscious for two days. The doctor has been here three times already. I spent all last night sitting here on this chair. You're not going to resign from the army. I am. Actually, that's not quite true. I'm going to get dismissed."

Dragan started to object but Celal silenced him with a stern look and leant back in his chair, making it creak. "We didn't bring you into the group just because you're a patriot. This country of ours may have plenty of traitors, but it has even more patriots. We need you, lieutenant. You. For Vesna Jevric."

Celal pulled his watch from his pocket. Opening the thick silver lid, he checked the time.

"Did you know that I'm from Prizren? Just like Lazar the monk. Do know who he was? No? He was an horologist. He made the clock for the first clock tower in Moscow. Spring-driven, all mechanical. A true work of genius. For two centuries it kept the time perfectly. Think about it, two whole centuries! Then they put in a new clock. And do you know what happened then? No? Of course you don't. Well, the clock tower burned down the very same day they changed the clock."

He closed the lid of his watch with a resounding "clack". Slipping the watch into his pocket, he crossed his legs. The small chair groaned under his weight.

"Vesna Jevric. She's one of Queen Draga's servants. A pretty girl. If you ask me, I think her lips are too thin, but still, she's pretty. If I remember rightly, she can speak three languages. When Queen Draga lied about being pregnant,

Vesna was in on it. The barren Queen was going to try to fool us by passing off her sister's child as her own. It's a good thing that not all Russians are as idiotic as those people who replaced Lazar's clock. Again and again I sent petitions to the Tsar explaining the situation, all in the most eloquent Russian, and in the end he sent his own physician down to investigate. The Queen can be as devilish as she wants, but she couldn't fool the physician. It was obvious that she wasn't pregnant. Because they didn't take my petitions seriously, the others were all caught off guard, including Apis. The King paid five doctors to sign a report saying that it was a phantom pregnancy. The Queen walked away with her name intact and we pretended to go along with it."

With those words he leapt to his feet and walked over to the wardrobe. He rummaged among the shelves and then tossed some clothes onto the bed. "Get dressed," he said. "An officer of your rank shouldn't be meeting a woman for the first time half-naked, especially a woman who is a servant at the palace. They'll be here soon."

Dragan reached out for his trousers and shirt.

"Captain," he said, "if this is about my committing suicide, I could dedicate the rest of my life to horology instead. I wouldn't mind."

"Dragan Petrovic, you truly are one of a kind. This country of ours has such a big heart that she doesn't even turn down the help of the biggest of fools."

9

The Doomed Palace

"Once upon a time a king was travelling through his lands, and as he gazed upon the Bojana River from the top of a hill, he caught sight of a rocky outcrop on the riverbank. 'There,' he said, 'is where I will build my palace.'

"So he summoned his two brothers to help him. One of them was a voivode who ruled over towns and vast fields, and his domain even included a mountain. The other brother was a cheerful, carefree man who brought joy to the hearts of others, but he spent much of his time alone writing under mulberry trees, the juice dripping from the berries staining the pages of poems that he never shared with anyone.

"When they received the summons, they set out to see their brother, one riding a bay horse and the other a sorrel horse.

"The king showed them the outcrop on the banks of the river where he planned to build his palace. The voivode and the poet were pleased with the king's decision and they promised to help him, for in those times even kings helped in the building of palaces. And so every day they toiled all day long, but in the morning they would see that their work lay in ruins."

Vesna paused for a moment and looked down at her nephew, who was lying on the divan with his head in her lap. Taking the book in her other hand, she went on reading:

"Years passed and every day it was the same. Everything they had built the day before would be lying in ruins. They posted sentries to watch over their work and they used only the finest stone, but all was in vain. One day before the break of dawn the king mounted his white horse and went down to keep watch over the foundation they had laid the day before. As the sun rose, the earth started rumbling and within seconds the foundation was reduced to rubble."

Vesna wrinkled her face and said, "Shall I read a different story? I'm getting a bit bored of this one." But the boy protested so vehemently that she turned back to the book.

"When the earth shook and rumbled, the king's horse reared up in fear, throwing the king to the ground. He rolled down the slope all the way to the water and his fine golden robe lined with badger fur was ripped and torn. Badly wounded, the king barely managed to pull himself out of the water. Just then a witch with hair down to her ankles emerged from the river. 'Vukavic, you are toiling in vain,' she said. Walking across the water towards the king, she added, 'The foundation is flawed. Even if you toil for a thousand days, you will find it in ruins every morning.'"

Vesna's expression betrayed her dislike for the tale.

Worried that the unhappy ending of the story would upset her nephew she decided to find another one, but just then someone knocked on the door.

Breathing a sigh of relief, she persuaded the boy to get up from her lap, and as she put the book on the bookshelf she recalled how much the story had frightened her as a child when her grandmother had read it to her. Those Germans, she thought, rewriting the story like that. Vesna had been translating the story from German to Serbian as she read.

Because she was a bit of a bookworm, Vesna was Queen Draga's favourite servant.

There were two more knocks, this time more insistent. Pulling a shawl over her shoulders, she hurried to the door, her nephew trailing at her heels as usual. Outside was none other than Radovan, the palace pastry chef, bowing deeply in greeting. He was wearing a pressed suit and his hair was neatly combed. The Radovan who cornered Dragan in the stairwell to tell him about the debauches at The Acorn was nothing like the man now standing before Vesna with the solemnity of a mansion butler.

Cordially, she invited him in.

Though it was a struggle, Dragan managed to put on the clothes that Celal had tossed on the bed. His stomach was growling but he breathed a sigh of relief when he saw Celal approaching with a bowl of soup.

"Albanian soup. Chicken, flour, yoghurt. You name it, it's in there. Normally it has garlic, too, but we wouldn't want to meet Vesna with garlic on our breath now, would we? Did you know that garlic is quite good for you? I sent a few petitions to the Ministry of Agriculture saying, 'Dear Minister, we should all eat garlic so that the people of our nation will be strong and vigorous.' I also wrote an anonymous newspaper article about it but all for naught. Still, it's always best not to eat garlic before meeting a woman for the first time, especially if she's the kind that can capture your heart with the ferocity of a vampire."

Celal sat on the edge of the bed and started feeding the young lieutenant with a crudely carved wooden spoon, filling it with large pieces of chicken and thick yoghurt broth with each scoop. Dragan was so hungry that he didn't mind the hot soup splashing onto his moustache as he slurped it down. Celal went on:

"Still, it would be wrong to call Vesna a vampire. Then again, for you, every woman is a vampire. You're a melancholic man, Dragan. People who don't know how to channel their power, their strength, become melancholic. And when that happens, you fall for every woman who walks into your life. For God's sake, don't chew with your mouth open!"

Because he was so concentrated on the soup, Dragan had heard little of what Celal was saying, but those last words sank in. Realizing the strangeness of the situation, Dragan picked up the spoon and, after carefully balancing the bowl on the mattress, quietly continued eating. Celal smiled.

"It tastes good, doesn't it? All it needs is some garlic… You see, lieutenant, the only solution for people who are born with a tendency to be melancholic is to keep themselves busy. If they don't, they fall in love as a way to cast off their depression, but when everything collapses they slip back into depression. So what do they do? They fall in love again. It's an endless cycle. Their depression is unlike other people's depression, just as their love is unlike others' love. Unfortunately, heavy-hearted people are unsuited to most work. In fact, melancholic people aren't good for much at all. Even when they do find something to keep themselves busy, it still comes to nothing."

Leaping up from the bed and nearly toppling over the bowl of soup in the process, Celal walked over to a coat that was hanging from a nail in the wall and took a book out of its pocket.

Rapidly Celal flipped through the pages like he'd read it a hundred of times. When he paused and cocked an eyebrow, Dragan surmised that he'd found what he was looking for.

"Since you're so prone to melancholy, do you think you can truly do it justice, Red Whiskers?" Celal asked.

He was fond of coming up with nicknames but, although he did so at every opportunity and believed they really hit the mark, none of them ever stuck.

Celal had been through a lot in his young life, and after leaving the attic flat on Skadar Street that day he would be tested by many more challenges in the years to come. But when death drew near he would be hounded by one regret, like a thirst that can never be slaked: the fact that no one ever retold his anecdotes and that his nicknames never stuck.

Dragan ate the last spoonful of soup and then lightly bit the spoon, pondering over the way he found the faint taste of wood so pleasant. After a pause just long enough for his earlier question to fade from Dragan's mind, Celal started reading aloud from the book:

"You're like a lighthouse shining beside the sea of humanity, motionless. All you can see is your own reflection in the water. You're alone, so you think it's a vast, magnificent panorama. You haven't sounded the depths. You simply believe in the beauty of God's creation. But I have spent all this time in the water, diving deep into the howling ocean of life, deeper than anyone. While you were admiring the surface, I saw the shipwrecks, the drowned bodies, the monsters of the deep."

Dragan sat up, ignoring his aching ribs. A gleam came into his eyes, brought on by both pain and the words he'd just heard. A tear ran down his cheek, washing a bit of chicken from his moustache, which he then started chewing pensively. Still feeling dizzy, he swayed ever so slightly.

Holding on to the table by the bed to steady himself, he murmured, "Alfred deee Mussey."

"Say his name again."

"Alfred deee Mussey."

"I know that you studied French but you have to get the accent right." Imitating Dragan's accent, he asked, "Which of Alfred deee Mussey's plays was that from?"

"*Lorenzaccio*, captain."

"Good. Maybe you're not as stupid as you'd like to be, or perhaps it's the effect of the soup… I have seen that soup drive soldiers who had wet themselves out of fear to fight for another hour. And not just a few soldiers, but a total of ninety-two. I cooked up the cauldron of soup myself. They tried to write me off as crazy. Crazy! If it had been up to the commanders, they would've shot those men for being deserters. But with my soup I saved the country ninety-two bullets and ninety-two brave men. True, I put garlic in that cauldron of soup, whole cloves as big as your thumb. Those piss-pants went on to fight roaring like lions, till they were hacking down the enemy with nothing but their bayonets. If I'd left it up to the commanders, we would have killed those chicken-hearted troops ourselves and we, not the enemy, would have fired those ninety-two bullets. Sure, they died, but they died as heroes."

One of Dragan's long eyelashes got in his eye. As he rubbed at it, he asked, "Which battle was that, captain?"

"It was a drill, Dragan. Which battle, ha! What is modern science all about? It's about arriving at material truths through experience."

As restless as if a watch inside him had suddenly sprung its gears, Celal started pacing the room, punctuating each sentence he spoke with a sigh.

"Very good, Dragan, very good. The book tells the story of Lorenzo, who killed Alessandro de' Medici, the Duke of Florence. That's narrow-minded dukes for you. So full of themselves!"

Tapping the cover of the book, which he'd placed on the table, he leant towards Dragan and said, "Vesna is going to be here in a few minutes. She's going to ask something of you and you're going to agree to it. She's touched by melancholy, just like you. But women's melancholy is different from men's. While men try to shake off their depression with love, women close themselves off to it and dedicate themselves to others. As for Vesna, she's devoted to her mother and especially Queen Draga. You two will get along well. You, young lieutenant, are going to rise up in the ranks. And not only that, my dear Petrovic, you will be a saint just like Saint Peter. We're going to sculpt your melancholy into a work of art. Both your patriotism and love will be rewarded. You will cast off your depression, and you will help Vesna break free from hers as well. Instead of being devoted to the Queen, she will be dedicated to you and her country. But there are three things you mustn't forget."

As if he were following orders, Dragan rose to his feet and, even though he was still holding the soup bowl, he stood at attention.

"*Primo*, when the time comes, you are going to say this quote from Alfred de Musset: 'How glorious it is—and also so painful—to be an exception.' You like that, don't you?

People who are afflicted with melancholy always think they are exceptions. The truth of the matter, however, is that there are no exceptions in life. There's at least two of everything. But I digress, that's a topic for another time… *Secundo*, you will make it seem that you are opposed to the coup. Wait, hear me out. Those who lie for the sake of their country speak the truth. That's a nice saying, isn't it? You are going to worm your way into the good graces of the King and Queen. *Tertio*, wait for news from me."

Popping open the silver lid of his watch, Celal checked the time. Then he walked backwards with measured steps, drew his sword and placed the tip against Dragan's neck, drawing a few drops of blood that trickled down the length of the blade. The bowl fell from Dragan's hand, clattering onto the floor, and a few droplets of the lieutenant's blood dripped onto the splattered soup.

Celal smiled.

Radovan came into the room, closing the door behind him.

After Vesna nodded in consent, he handed a small box to the child. "It's raspberry cake. I put in two almond biscuits as well, but save those for later. I made them for the King and Queen last night, and they loved them. The Queen summoned me and said, 'Radovan, during these bitter times, you manage to sweeten life up.'" After her nephew ran off to the kitchen, Vesna sat down on the divan. Speaking as if delivering a report, Radovan said, "The lieutenant who lives in the attic flat seems to be a good candidate for a guardsman. I've been keeping an eye on him since he moved in. Not once has he lost his composure, even when I told him the most impertinent of tales. He's a quiet, introverted man. He may look like a bit of a weakling but our contacts in the secret police said that he got good marks at the military academy. He's tough, despite his refinement, and he's a good, open-minded patriot. He shuns radical ideas and he is fond of reading."

Vesna adjusted the shawl on her shoulders and motioned for Radovan to sit down. Chin cupped in her hand, she thought for a few moments and said, "Radovan, the Queen trusts you. Did you know that your cakes are the only thing that she doesn't have her food taster try first? That's how much she trusts you. Everyone in the palace is on edge. Something's going on. Do you remember that Apis was at the head of the procession when the King and Queen got married? But these days he goes around calling the Queen filthy names. You see, they can't remove him from his post because they fear that the army will revolt. That's why they decided to change the guards, every single one of them. Well, I suppose you know about that already, what am I going on about? I'm so tired, Radovan. If you say he's a good candidate, so be it. But I should meet this lieutenant first. If he's as good as you say, let's take him on as a guard."

"Actually, there's more. You mentioned that your nephew needs a tutor. The lieutenant speaks fluent French and he also dabbles in history. He could give French and history lessons to your nephew. But, of course, you should decide after speaking with him."

Vesna's face lit up.

"His mother did leave his education in my hands… When can I meet this lieutenant?"

"Now, if you'd like. He should be at home, according to the note a doctor sent to his unit. We could wish him well and talk about the lessons." Radovan checked his watch. "With your permission, let's go now while your nephew is in the kitchen."

"This country of ours must really be in trouble if a pastry chef and a servant are choosing the palace guards."

For the first time since he had come into the room Radovan's features softened. Leaning down, he said in hushed tones, "Apis is the head of military intelligence and you are the head of the Queen's intelligence network. I can say this, my dear Vesna Jevric, because I know both of you. If I were still a gambling man, I'd put all my money on you."

Vesna laughed and got to her feet.

"Very well, then, let's go now. I can tell that you are eager to introduce us."

As they walked towards the door, Radovan said, "There's one more thing. Apis's men gave the lieutenant a rather severe beating. That's why the physician went to see him. At first I was hesitant about taking him on as a guard, but when I found out about that all my doubts vanished. His loyalties are certain to lie with you. It's good that we're going to see him now, before Apis's men get their hands on him again."

"What's the lieutenant's name?"

"Dragan. Dragan Petrovic."

Dragan hadn't yet noticed that his blood was trickling down the blade of the sword pressed against his throat. He merely stood there, mouth agape, staring at Celal, who was still smiling. There was a roaring in his ears and his vision was blurry. He gave up on trying to make sense of what was happening.

Dragan was like a piece of wood being tossed hither and thither on a raging sea. He was like the leg of a table that was now nothing more than a stick of firewood, or perhaps the tiny rudder of a forgotten toy boat that had broken into pieces. His meaningless, piteous life had taken a preposterous turn and he was helpless in the face of it all.

When Radovan and Vesna reached the top of the stairs, they found the door ajar. Radovan nudged it open with his foot.

Celal was standing in a dramatic pose, blood dripping down the blade of his sword, which was still pressed against Dragan's throat. Vesna screamed.

As Radovan charged at him, Celal murmured, "Right on time."

At that moment Dragan did the most sensible thing, given the situation in which he found himself: he fainted.

10

The Death of a Corpse

"I WAS EXPECTING to get arrested but I never thought that I'd be here for two whole days, Colonel. For a moment I was worried that the uprising would start devouring its own children before it even got started, just like Saturn, which would have upset me, naturally. Not out of concern for myself, you understand, but because it would've been a sign that the uprising had failed. History shows that uprisings start with a spirit of solidarity, but custom dictates that once they have achieved success they devour their children. An uprising that breaks with custom cannot be a true uprising. Nothing good can be expected of an uprising that doesn't lead to revolution…

"At least that's what I learnt at the military academy in France.

"In any case, I see now that you don't think I was planning to overthrow you and, in fact, you weren't planning on devouring me. And you were right on both counts. *Primo*, I don't think that I would be very tasty. *Secundo*, I don't have my sights set on anyone's position. *Tertio*, it would have been a bit perfidious given that I'd just succeeded in setting the lieutenant on the path to becoming a guard at the palace."

Apis sat there listening to Celal, looking at him disdainfully. "I wonder if it's really a good idea to bring in the new king from France," he said. "I can only hope that he's not a rubbish-spouting babbler like you. Fuck off, captain. And your Saturn and Jupiter, too, for that matter. Don't go around shouting your head off, someone will hear you. What did you think you were doing, spouting off about plans for an uprising like a blathering pimp from Paris in the courtyard of the damn military prison!" Grabbing Celal by the arm and standing on tiptoes, Apis pushed his nose close to his face and growled, "Captain, watch yourself. Watch yourself very closely. Everyone's expendable, especially uppity types like you. With a single look I can fuck you over so bad that you'll think you've been buggered by a porcupine. Pray for two things. Pray that the French end of the uprising holds together and that Karageorgevic comes through. We need him."

After settling back on his heels, Apis loosed his grip on Celal's arm and then let go completely. As he headed towards the exit of the military prison with Celal in tow, two soldiers at the gate saluted him. After hesitating for a moment, the soldier on the right broke his salute and opened the gate. Apis and Celal stepped into a gleaming carriage waiting outside.

"Colonel, what's the second thing I should pray for?"

"Isn't that enough, Celal Bey? Are you really serious about being part of the Serbian army? To all appearances you've done well in taking on your role. You can speak openly here. The driver can't hear us."

"That's all fine but what's the second issue? If the soldiers on patrol are loyal to the King and Queen, we won't get all of the intelligence we need because they won't talk to anyone from the resistance."

The ends of Apis's moustache quivered ever so slightly as he exhaled through his nose.

"I was going to say that you should pray for sunny weather. Everyone knows that fine weather puts me in good spirits. Just like everyone else, the soldiers at the prison are loyal to me and our mission, not to that whore or her errand-boy king. If they're going to stay loyal, they have to see me being hard on new recruits like you."

"I think we're clear on that. Even I was convinced. But how are you going to convince Vesna that I've been dismissed?"

"That's easy. You wounded a low-ranking lieutenant, a crime that falls under the military's jurisdiction. Since I'm the head of military intelligence, there are various measures I can take. Demotion, a salary cut, an official warning, and so on. They all fit the bill. And after the superb show you put on we had no trouble getting the lieutenant signed on as a guard. He started work the very next day. Well done, Celal Bey. You found the right man for the job, convinced him to take it on, and secured Vesna's trust in him, meaning the Queen's trust. But that's the end of it. Of course, you understand that we cannot let it be known that a Turk was involved in the uprising. You did your job. When our mutual friend sent you to us, I had a lot of doubts but he held up his end of the deal. And so will we."

They stopped at the edge of a neighbourhood where the city's grand buildings gave way to huts with roofs no higher than the head of the horse pulling the carriage. Apis leant across Celal and opened the door.

"Walk down the road between those two shacks for about ten minutes and you'll see your people from the circus. You've done your part, we'll handle the rest. Enjoy the rest of your time in Belgrade."

With one foot still on the carriage step, Celal turned to Apis and said, "Colonel, it's not a sunny day."

"Well, then find something else to pray for, Celal Bey."

Celal made his way down the hill gnawing the inside of his cheek as he butchered a tongue-twister that he couldn't quite remember. Rain started pattering down on the road.

When it's raining, do you get wetter if you walk slowly or if you run? The question was moot on streets as muddy as those. In no time at all the soles of Celal's boots were coated in a thick layer of earth, making it difficult for him to walk, let alone run, so he picked up a stick lying by the side of the road and used it to guide himself through what was now practically a river of mud. He started singing the few lyrics he could remember from an old Celali brigand shanty:

"They will hunt you down no matter where you go / Not even a hundred prayers will save your soul / They strung them up one by one / And skinned Mehdi who was on the run."

"What if," he thought, "I just up and died in some unknown place, like on a miserable muddy slope. Or what if one of Apis's thugs, or one the Queen's men, laid me out with a bullet to the back of my head in a remote corner of the city. There I'd be, wearing the uniform of a foreign army, dead."

He was so distracted that the stick slipped from his grasp but at the same time he was overcome by a feeling of peacefulness that he'd never experienced before. When the rain started pouring down, he remembered the rest of the song and sang it at the top of his voice.

The run-down shacks lining the road started thinning out. At one point Celal looked around and realized that he was in the middle of a field, up to his knees in mud as the rain hammered down. He pressed on. Through the curtain of rain he spotted a rocky knoll in the distance and headed in that direction. The knoll appeared and disappeared in the deluge of rain like a fairy-tale castle, and just when he thought that he still had a way to go, he found himself at the foot of it. He clambered to the top.

Despite the rain, the earth was firm. Atop that solid soil were four hooves, and above the hooves a majestic horse.

Seated on the horse was a hooded rider wearing a hunting jacket.

The rider signalled and Celal clambered onto the horse. As they set off, the horse's hooves skipping over the water, Celal held on to the rider's slender body.

"They will make your life a misery / So leave off your wicked ways / Crows will devour you one day / As your fame and glory fade away."

"We haven't put up the main tent yet. But you should see it, Celal, it's magnificent. It would be a bit of a squeeze but you could fit a whole town in there. They were awestruck in Vienna. And you know the Viennese, they are hardly ever in awe of anything. All they know is theatre and classical music. Even the high-school pupils—almost all of them are set on becoming art critics. Pale-faced runts as short as toy soldiers. Their parents are just fatter versions of them, and less scrupulous, too. But we bewitched them all, children and adults alike. Even aristocrats came and watched the monkey acrobatics, mouths agape as if they were watching an Ibsen play. The tent was packed for weeks on end. If we were to set it up again, the tent would echo with German cries of astonishment once more. That's how well it went."

Céline stopped and looked at Celal as he sat on a stool in his muddy uniform trying to warm himself with a blanket thrown over his shoulders. She tossed a few logs into the stove beside him and closed the lid halfway with a pair of tongs.

"But Celal, you were only told to infiltrate the coup plotters, not bring yourself to ruin. Look at yourself. Why don't you take up acting on the Vienna stage? You'd be a star."

Celal said nothing in reply. First he took off his muddy boots, and then his pants. After wrapping the blanket around his waist, he dragged the stool closer to the stove.

"I hope there's someone who does laundry in this circus. I need to wash my uniform. I might need it again sometime."

"Tomorrow you can give it to the stable boy. He takes cares of those things along with the horses."

"Very well."

The fire crackled and they fell silent.

Céline took off her hunting jacket and ran her fingers through her hair. Then she sat down at the dressing table with her back to Celal and started brushing her hair in the mirror.

Even though the stove was already filled with wood, Celal shoved in another piece, choking the flames. A thin, dark trail of smoke wafted from the stove into the room. Using the tongs, Celal poked the wood around until it started burning again and the smoke started going up the chimney. He met Céline's gaze in the mirror.

"The cut on my palm hasn't healed yet."

"Probably because you didn't want it to. Which means you didn't miss me," Céline said with a wink. "But I still rescued you like a knight in shining armour when I pulled you up onto my horse just now. I think you got carried away with playing soldier and you didn't want me to come along and spoil your fun, so you didn't let it heal. You knew if it did, that would mean the time for our reunion was drawing near."

"Céline, you couldn't be more wrong. I think you missed me so much you couldn't bear to wait any longer."

"Celal, please. More than enough time has passed for a little cut to heal."

"Well, now that we're together again, I hope it heals up. If I'm going to be a secret agent, I certainly don't want to have any scars that'll give me away."

"It's nice to see that you're so excited about being a spy."

"Stop that rubbish. Why did you stay in Vienna so long?"

Céline handed him a towel so that he could dry his hair.

"We never got news that a revolt was breaking out. And while we're not strong enough yet to stir up a revolution that will take down the Habsburgs, as I told you, we were able to gather intelligence up there. It's shocking—people are suspicious of everyone and everything these days, but when they go to the circus they're suddenly as naïve as newborn babes. I'm sure we found out more about the Empire than Emperor Franz Joseph himself knows."

Céline got up and tossed Celal an open-collared lace-up shirt. He took off his uniform and asked, as he pulled the shirt over his head, "Have you heard anything from Sahir?"

"We met a few times at his place in Vienna. He stayed for about a week. He was in such a good mood that his eyes even cleared up a bit. Well, as good a mood as Sahir can be in. Any particular reason why you asked?"

"Not at all. I hardly heard anything from you, so how could I ask any loaded questions?"

"You know, Celal, reproach is unattractive in a man, especially when it is underhanded. I always took you to be the kind of person who speaks his mind."

"Okay, maybe there was a particular reason for my question. I've been here for months now. Does Sahir really think that people like Apis are going to bring peace to the world? I'm starting to have doubts."

"To tell you the truth, I'm not sure myself what he wants any more. But based on what he said in Vienna, he seems hopeful about the intelligence we've gathered. Emperor Franz Joseph knows that a revolt is in the works in Serbia, but he's happy to let it go ahead. He thinks that if the uprising fails, it will bring the Serbian King and Queen closer to him. On the other hand, if it succeeds, he thinks that he'll be able to bring the new king Karageorgevic under his influence, too. He'd probably try to buy him off by giving the Serbs in Bosnia some autonomy, or by selling him cheap munitions. At least, that's what he said. Oh, and he said this, too: 'Thank Celal for me. He did a splendid job.'"

"So what are we going to do now?"

"We're going to teach you some circus acts. The show's going to start soon. By the way, I hope you're not afraid of lions."

"I don't take myself seriously enough to be afraid of anything."

"Now you're the one talking rubbish. A man who doesn't take himself seriously wouldn't assume a fake identity and meddle with conspiracies in a foreign city just for the sake of changing world history. Or stick his head into a lion's mouth, for that matter."

"My lady, may I point out that you hadn't mentioned that last part before?"

"Don't worry, it's a well-trained lion. Its teeth have been filed down and they've got rubber caps."

"Being comforted like that is worrying in itself."

"See, you do take yourself seriously. While you work on your routine I'm going to meet up with my penfriend Vesna. Sahir's orders."

"If Vesna's in on the job, why did I spend months working to get Dragan taken on as a guard?"

"She's not in on it. But if the revolt fails, we may need a way to influence the King and Queen. Sahir thinks that Karageorgevic is a better choice for bringing democracy to Serbia, but he also said that if Apis and his revolution don't succeed, the King and Queen might be persuaded to at least let the people have some say in the running of the country. Now, we know that the Queen likes to write and draw. She's even had a few articles and stories published in foreign magazines under an assumed name. Vesna submits the pieces for her. So, recently Sahir started a literary magazine in France. It's actually quite decent. Even those snobby high-school children in Vienna who don't like anything can't put it down. I'm going to meet up with Vesna as the magazine's representative and tell her that I'm doing a tour of Europe to promote it. So as you can see, whether the revolt happens or not, Sahir has a plan."

The rain and wind started to die down, and the small room was warming up as the stove crackled.

Celal got up and approached Céline. Taking the brush from her hand, he started brushing her hair, which he then stroked with his wounded hand. He ran his fingers over her shoulders and leant down to kiss her neck. Then he reached around and pressed the wound on his palm to her lips. At first she nibbled at it, but her bites got harder and harder.

Céline spun around, pulled her skirt up to her waist and spread her legs. Grabbing Celal by the hair, she pushed his head down. Celal fell to his knees.

Placing his bloodied hand on the floor, he tried to push himself up so that he could kiss Céline but she held him down. Their first kiss was worthy of Şerif Bey's erotic books.

Celal was unable to shake off the nightmare he'd had.

Not even the storm raging outside could rouse him.

Nor the stove, which was now cold.

When someone started knocking on the door, he opened his eyes. The knocks were quick raps at first, and then became more insistent. He ran his hand along the top of the mattress under the warm blanket.

When the knocking got so hard that it seemed the door would fly off its hinges, he leapt out of bed, put on a shirt and wrapped the blanket around his waist. He opened the door.

The wind swung it open, slamming it against the wall outside.

Céline was standing there with a blond man of average height, with a drooping moustache. They quickly came inside to get out of the wind. Celal struggled to get the door closed, and when at last he managed it he saw that the man was lighting the stove. When the stove was burning steadily enough to warm up the room again, the man got up and kissed Céline's hand with exaggerated pomp.

With the same affected air, he presented her with a box of sweets and a bouquet of violets. As she was setting the gifts aside, the guest approached Celal and, placing his hands on his shoulders, pulled him in for a tight embrace. Stunned, Celal stepped back and held out his hand. They shook. With his index fingers, the guest wiped away the water dripping from his hair to his eyebrows.

Céline motioned for the two men to sit down.

The guest popped a chocolate into his mouth and offered one to Celal. As he sucked on the chocolate, the guest said in a hoarse voice, "The name's Celal, right? I hope you'll be able to follow what I'm about to tell you. As you know, time can be a restless thing, unlike history, which is quite prone to laziness. And when time begins to fly too fast, history can't keep up. It just looks on at the merry-go-round of time as it whirls round and round... And in the end it's all too much. History gives up and collapses on a chair. It becomes so lazy, so very very lazy, that it doesn't even bother to repeat itself. And you know, Celal, I think that is how we can spot moments of historical significance: when the whirl of time stops the repetition of history. Did you see what Count Zeppelin did? Two years ago, he filled a huge sack with hydrogen at Lake Constance and flew up into the air. I saw it with my very own eyes. It was nothing like a hot-air balloon. Let me put it this way: if a hot-air balloon is a rowing boat, von Zeppelin's creation was a frigate. Of course, history knows nothing of frigates soaring through the air, and so as it looked on it started to feel dizzy, and now it has stopped repeating itself. But we shouldn't put much faith in the pauses of history. The important question is: how will the Zeppelin be used? To whisk letters across the Atlantic to America? To drop bombs on battle lines? If it's the latter, then we'll know that history has got used to the merry-go-round, sat up in its chair and started repeating itself again. It's those moments that matter."

The guest undid his wig-clips and tossed his blond wig on the floor. Reaching down, he picked up a leather bag that was sitting between his legs and held it out to Celal.

"Here's your money. Please forgive me for upsetting you with that disappearing act and causing you so much trouble."

Scratching his beard, Celal took the bag and tossed it on the bed beside him. He got to his feet and looked at the wig for a while, and then he picked up one of the clips to examine it. When the silence became unbearable, he said, "Jean, is this some kind of vaudeville act? What need is there for all these shenanigans: the wig, the empty chatter, as if you were trying to dupe a villager at the county fair. Is this the time or place for games? You come here and ramble on about history, repetition, and how Count Zeppelin flew off into the sky… And to top it off, the two of you were in cahoots, preparing this surprise for me as if I was some kind of aristocrat fallen on hard times who needs some entertainment on his deathbed. Jean, I rarely get upset. Very rarely. And I never know what's going to upset me. But when I heard that you'd been killed, I was devastated. What was I to you? Just some Ottoman gentleman writing tasteless yet saleable stories? A sucker? As if that wasn't enough, you seem to think that I'm so exotic that you can put me on display in the circus. Is that how it is? Am I just a stranger to you, expected to make do with whatever information you see fit to pass on to me? Am I no more than a loyal fool doing your bidding? A mere nobody to be swallowed up by your lofty schemes? A monkey wearing a fez? Jean, I need you to tell me something. Please understand, I'm not threatening or blackmailing you. Maybe I really am a loyal servant. If not, I'd be even angrier than I already am. I'm not sure. But I would like to know what's going on. Tell me, please. As an equal. What's happening? And, more importantly, why?"

Celal stared at Jean, his stern gaze demanding a reply.

Jean slowly shook his head. "I'm sorry, Celal," he said. "I suppose that I thought you would see the funny side of it all. But I was wrong. It's my fault. When I'm feeling uneasy, I become blind to what other people are feeling. I hope you can forgive me."

Celal cupped his chin in his hands and leant forward. "You haven't changed at all, Jean. At school, when you sliced open that poor boy's face during fencing practice you didn't feel an ounce of pity for him. True, you stood there in shock and the first words out of your mouth were, 'My apologies, please forgive me.' But the fact is, you were using a real foil, not one of the practice ones. I may have said I wasn't threatening you, but I'd recommend that you explain yourself before I change my mind. I'm starting to have second thoughts about holding back my anger."

"You'll restrain yourself. You always have. That 'poor boy', as you called him, was also using a real foil. Yes, I asked him to forgive me, but not for the reason you think. We used to call him 'the blond fibber', and his nickname for you was 'the Sultan's whore'. He used to go around saying that all you wanted was to get your hands on a huge French cock. You were new at school and, if you recall, I was the only person who would talk to you. I'll admit, I only objected to what he was saying because I didn't want people to gossip about me, not because I wanted to defend you. When I cut his face open like that, I felt bad for agreeing to fence with him, and I still feel bad."

Celal walked over to the dressing table and returned holding a small mirror, a blusher brush and a piece of soap, and then he poured some water from a pitcher into a small metal bowl, which he set on the stove. When the bowl started steaming, he set it on the side table. He picked up a piece of flower-patterned cloth hanging beside the table and wound it around his neck. After putting the soap into the water, he used the brush to whip it into foam, which he then lathered onto his face. Looking intently into the mirror, he started shaving his unkempt beard with slow, even strokes.

Whistling, Celal carefully shaved every inch of his face and then unwound the now soaking-wet piece of cloth from his neck. He tossed it on the ground and used it to meticulously wipe up the hair on the floor. Satisfied with his handiwork, he stood up, walked over to Jean, and gave him a slap that sent him sprawling to the floor, his head colliding with a side table as he fell, knocking out two teeth.

Still furious, Celal turned to Céline and took two firm steps towards her. In return he received two resounding slaps across his freshly shaved cheeks. Céline rushed over to Jean, taking his head in her arms and dabbing with her scarf at the blood oozing from his mouth.

His cheeks burning, Celal sat back down on the bed and looked at Jean.

"He used to call me 'the Sultan's whore'?"

Jean lifted his head from Céline's lap, got up and lowered himself into a chair, heaving a sigh as he undid the top buttons of his shirt. He reached out and picked up the mirror, which he set on his chest and started using to examine his mouth, occasionally glancing up at Celal. Rubbing his cheek, he felt around in his mouth with his tongue, probing the gaps where the two teeth had once been, and then lowered the mirror to his lap.

Céline walked to the door and opened it. Over the roar of the wind blowing in from outside, she shouted, "We don't have much time, so you two finish up your pissing competition," and then she walked out and slammed the door behind her.

The two men sat in silence, avoiding each other's gaze. After a while Celal got up and walked towards the kitchen. "I'm going to make coffee," he said. "There's cognac and glasses over there. Pour us some."

"I'd say that for a Sultan's whore you like to order people around too much."

"Well, I'd like to kill you but we don't always get our way in life."

"If everything goes according to plan, no one's going to want to kill anyone else ever again."

"I wouldn't make such grand statements if I were you."

"Well, according to the official records I'm a dead man, so I'd say that I have every right to say anything I want. Celal, you must understand that I had to hide. There's no better way to hide than to die, and it's even better if you are murdered. But if your body isn't found, that's a problem because they might come looking for you. So when I had to go into hiding, a corpse was needed. I paid off the gambling debt of a janitor at the medical school, and he agreed to tell me when a body came in that would be a good match for me. I waited for two months. When a suitable body finally showed up, I had the janitor put on a fake beard and we took the money out of the account you and I shared. Then we dressed up the body in some of my clothes, put my identity papers in his pocket, and shot him in the face… It never occurred to me that you would be so upset."

Jean reached into his left pocket and pulled out a revolver.

"You weren't part of the plan, Celal. Sure, it's touching that you were so moved by my death, but why did you come all the way to France instead of enjoying your life as an aristocrat in Istanbul?"

Celal rushed angrily towards Jean, but the Frenchman held the revolver steadily in two hands, aimed at Celal.

"I'm sure that we can work something out, Celal. It'd be easy for you to convince me of anything you want. But if you take one more step, I'll have no choice but to shoot you, at least in the leg, and there's no need for that. Just tell me why you're here in Belgrade working at a circus. I'm sure there's a logical explanation."

"Guns aren't your style, Jean. So calm down. And don't worry—I'm not going to try anything. The cack-handed way you're holding that gun tells me that even if you tried to shoot me in the leg, you'd probably put a bullet through the middle of my forehead by mistake. Yes, there is a logical explanation for my being here. An angel's trumpet hookah pipe in fact! Actually there are a lot of reasons for my being here. If Karachiyano hadn't crossed my path when I was drunk, we wouldn't have had that wrestling match. If I hadn't smoked that hookah laced with angel's trumpet, I wouldn't have hallucinated and lost, and I wouldn't have been forced to leave the city and go to Marseille. But that still doesn't explain why I'm here. When I found out that my dear friend Jean had been killed and was questioned by the police, I decided to go to Paris even though I was penniless. After a few stops here and there, I ended up in this place. If you hadn't disappeared and taken off with my money, I'd be in Marseille right now living it up and writing more stories. So, Jean, I suggest you carefully put that gun back into your pocket before you shoot me or shoot yourself by accident, and then tell me why you had to fake your own death. It's your turn to answer the question you asked me. Why are you here, Jean?"

Jean smiled and murmured, "So, it was Karachiyano…" and then slipped the gun back into his pocket.

"Celal, you're here because of Sahir, and I had to die because of him. But I never thought that you'd get tangled up in this too. Karachiyano works for the Italian consulate as a translator, right? It's a cover. He's actually a gunrunner,

145

but working at the consulate helps him get things through customs. A clever swindler, that one. And seeing as he drove you out of Istanbul, you've probably worked that out, too. Sahir got it in his head to involve you. You see, Karachiyano works for Sahir as well, meaning that he's the reason you're here, not me. Ah, Celal, it's like we're all part of a big family that doesn't get along. You were just a distant relative until recently, but now you're a fully fledged member."

"Were you really going to shoot me?"

"No, it's just a toy gun. A circus prop."

"For once I'd like for something to be real."

"My story is real for the most part. And it seems like it's going to continue with all of us. You, me, Sahir, Céline. We're all part of the same family that was pulled together by Arif and Pierre. A family bound to the peace machine. You were outside the family, because Arif had given up on the peace machine when you saved his life. He'd never been convinced that it was a good idea to meddle with people's free will and he thought that it was a sign when you came into his life. He once said, 'If a child can take down a bull, humanity can achieve peace through its own free will.' Still, he and Pierre stayed in touch by letter. When Arif was thinking about sending you to France to study, he asked Pierre for his opinion. Pierre recommended that he send you to the school I was attending, as did my mother and father. You see, Monsieur Pierre was my uncle."

Celal found a pair of trousers in the closet from which Céline had taken the shirt she'd given him. Pulling off the blanket wrapped around his waist, he put the trousers on and then refilled Jean's empty glass.

"So it would seem that being an orphan has its advantages. Why didn't you ever tell me any of this?"

"Every family has its secrets, Celal. And I didn't know about many of them myself until just recently. I was working for Sahir but I knew nothing about Arif or the peace machine. Sahir isn't fond of entertainment but he enjoys the business of entertainment. Sahir and I were in charge of printing and distributing your books, and he also runs the photography studio. These days he's developed a taste for cinema. His latest idea is to turn some of your books into films and show them at brothels—for a fee, of course—to get the clients excited. You have to admit, it's a brilliant idea. Sahir is involved in thousands of other things. I was in charge of the erotic book and nightlife end of his business. It wasn't a great life but I wasn't complaining much. If Céline hadn't got that letter when she turned twenty-one, I probably would've gone on getting by in life and you would've made a small fortune with your books."

Celal reached out and rummaged through his leather bag. "You might be right," he said. "But why did you disappear with all the money?"

"Because of the letter. Also perhaps because of my foolishness. Probably a bit of both. Isn't that how it usually is?"

"For you, you mean."

"Isn't everything that happens the result of various causes? I'm no exception to the rule."

"That doesn't change the fact that you're foolish."

"Fine, you've got me there. The notary's clerk delivered the letter. My uncle Pierre had entrusted a letter to the notary with the instructions that it was to be delivered to her on Céline's twenty-first birthday. And what a letter it was… We found out that Sahir wasn't really an orphan whom Pierre had met during one of his excursions. We also learnt that neither Arif Bey nor you were what you seemed. I mean, we always knew that you were strong, but how could a boy take down a bull?"

"If you don't slow down and fill in the details I'm going to take *you* down any second now."

"Patience, my friend, patience. It was more like a book than a letter. It explained everything: his conversations with Arif, Sahir, his experiments… Of course it was mostly about the peace machine. It was filled with details—formulas, drawings, you name it. The letter was like an instruction manual."

"I saw a model of the machine at Sahir's place in Paris."

"But you didn't see it work—because it doesn't work. Rather, the one that Sahir has doesn't work. So we mentioned the letter to Sahir, except for the part about the drawings."

"Why?"

"Celal, you just knocked out my teeth and now you want to interrogate me?"

Jean walked over to the window and looked outside.

"The wind's dying down. Let's go out. We can talk about the rest of this with Céline. Isn't it true that families have secrets, but that at the same time everything's out in the open?"

Using the clips, they put Jean's wig back on. He pointed to the bushy moustache that covered his upper lip. "It's still there despite the slap you gave me. The glue I used is extraordinary."

"That's just great."

"Aren't you going to be cold?"

Celal opened the door. It swung open easily in the light breeze. "So who's going to play the characters in the films based on my books?"

"I, of course, now that I've mastered the art of wigs and fake moustaches."

Celal paused in the doorway. "And Céline?"

Jean popped a piece of chocolate into his mouth, and as he left he muttered, "Come on, Celal, I thought you would've worked out by now that she's more interested in directing."

"I drank pear brandy / And passed over the railway bridge / Arriving at truth's abode... Pear brandy, plum brandy, cherry brandy, fig brandy, peach brandy, even grape brandy. The spirits aren't so bad here. It would seem that these gentlemen have settled their quarrel. That's something to celebrate, so come on, boys."

Céline was sitting at a wooden table in a tall, broad circus wagon. She held out two glasses. Jean stepped into the wagon and sat down opposite Céline. In a single gulp he downed the drink she'd offered him.

"You know, Celal, it's a bit like Calvados."

"You shouldn't drink it so quickly."

"Celal's been here a long time. You should listen to him."

With that, Céline downed her own glass, which had been filled to the brim, and then poured and drank another.

"Then again, speed is a relative concept. Celal, don't just stand there. Come in and have a seat so that we can drink to your rekindled friendship."

He sat down and twirled his glass of apple brandy. After taking a measured sip, he swished the brandy around in his mouth and swallowed it.

Jean pulled from his pocket a small glass vial containing a white powder. Pressing the thumb and forefinger of his right hand together, he shook some of the powder into the gap between his fingers and sniffed it up his nose with a quick snort. The whites of his eyes suddenly glowed and he turned to Céline and Celal with a smile, launching into a monologue that lasted for hours, whipped on as he was by the snorts he took, one after another.

As Jean explained and explained, Celal and Céline drank and drank.

Celal's mind recorded all that Jean said. "Recorded" is perhaps not the right word; he processed what he was hearing, but in the end, even though his mind was still in full control of his body, Celal had become little more than a stone, a very heavy stone that Céline seemed to be hewing and shaping with her gaze. Céline's eyes seared his flesh as they moved across his body, filling him with a throbbing pain.

Jean explained that Sahir was actually a gun merchant after nothing but money, and that, as business had expanded, his companies had signed deals with certain governments to keep them in power. He then said that Şerif Efendi's books had inspired him to set up a prostitution empire that he ran by means of blackmail, drawing people into his inescapable web of intrigue, and that there wasn't a minister, parliamentarian or business owner who wasn't in Sahir's pocket, either directly or through Jean.

Jean said, "We'll activate the peace machine on the opening night of the circus, when no one's expecting it—especially not Sahir."

Jean tapped the remaining powder onto his moistened finger, which he then rubbed on his gums.

"If you're with me, we'll turn it on during the first show."

Celal ran his fingers across Céline's waist. She smiled at Jean and said, "Get out." Jean obediently got up and left.

Celal ceased to be a stone, as he touched her and rediscovered his body.

His hands, the hands of a blind man, drew Céline in the darkness of his mind.

I I

The Circus Dervish

THE QUEEN'S DELUSIONS

SPECTRE OF REVOLT IN BELGRADE

Telegram from our local correspondent

LONDON, 3RD MAY 1903

King Alexander, who married his mother's lady-in-waiting despite the protests of the National Assembly members, was recently overjoyed to hear that his marriage had been blessed with a child. However, it has since emerged that he had been deceived by the Queen's delusions. It is not yet clear whether the Queen deliberately deceived the King or was the victim of a hysterical episode. Regardless, preparations for celebration in Serbia had been made for nothing.

Dr Stegireff had publicly expressed doubts that the Queen was with child, whereupon, in an attempt to reassure the King and Queen, Dr Caulet accused Dr Stegireff of being an incompetent fool. The Tsar, aware of the ongoing dispute between the two physicians, demanded an inquiry into the matter.

On the orders of the Tsar, Dr Wertheim, a resident of Vienna, and Dr Kantakuzen, a resident of Bucharest, examined the Queen and reported that she had not been guilty of ill intentions, had truly believed that she was with child, and was suffering from an inflammation of the uterus. If my sources are correct, it appears that it will be difficult for the Queen to fulfil the King's hopes.

On hearing of this latest development, the people of Serbia, already disgruntled with the Queen, have become even more indignant, and it is said that the military has begun to seriously consider the possibility of a revolt for the sake of the citizenry.

Alongside Queen Draga's "hysterical episodes", a new law which determines that on the King's death the crown will pass to the Queen's brother has prompted a rumour that a group of army officers is preparing to overthrow the King and place the exiled Peter Karageorgevic on the throne in his stead.

THE SHARP SCENT of spirits lingering in the air seared Dragan's nostrils, bringing tears to his eyes. The translation of the article had been printed in faint ink on the newspaper's yellowed onion-skin paper, and some of the letters were illegible.

For those who read the story, the phantom pregnancy was a relatively easy riddle to solve. Vesna gently pushed the newspaper across the table towards Dragan, who said that he'd already read it. She got up and walked to the window, the frame of which was freshly varnished. When he saw her struggling to open it, Dragan leapt up to help. As Vesna tried to turn the handle, his hand brushed her fingers, sending a jolt of shame through him. He recoiled as if he'd just been slapped across the face. The embarrassment of knowing that Vesna had read the article merged with the shame he felt at so tactlessly touching her hand, and he staggered backwards.

"I'm sorry, it's that strange smell in the air. I felt dizzy for a moment."

After momentarily struggling with the sash window, she managed to slide it up and secure it in place with brass tabs on either side of the frame. A light breeze wafted into the large room, which was in the palace's east wing.

"So the Queen doesn't really care what they say about her."

"Quite to the contrary. She may be a commoner by birth, but don't think that her nobility isn't real just because she acquired it by marriage. Anyone who can stand tall in the face of adversity is noble, and that's how the Queen is. But this has really upset her. That story first ran in an Australian newspaper. Can you imagine it, lieutenant? The whole world is talking about whether or not our Queen is with child."

"It's a shameful state of affairs."

"Yes, but only for the people who write rubbish like that. And for those people who jump at every opportunity to try to overthrow the King. It's shameful that they try to find scapegoats for their own ineptitude, and take their anger out on the palace just because their lives haven't turned out the way they wanted. They'll won't rest until the Queen is buried. I'm telling you, lieutenant, it truly is most shameful."

Dragan eased himself into a chair near the window. Both his thoughts and movements were sluggish, and he felt like a clumsy giant who is vanquished by a child in a fairy tale. The breeze gently blowing through the half-open window ruffled Vesna's hair, which was set aglow by the light streaming in, and Dragan suddenly found himself biting his lip as he gazed at her. He sat there in silence, gnawing at his lip until he tasted the saltiness of blood.

"Well, my dear Vesna, what's done is done. I know it's not my place to speak on the matter, but I wonder if it might not be better if the Queen were to take a trip abroad. Or, at the very least, the King and Queen could stop hosting guests at the palace for a while until everything settles down. Maybe then the Queen would produce an heir."

The thought of how the Queen was being slandered filled Vesna with a fresh sense of rage that coursed through her entire body. Taking a few steps towards Dragan, she said, "You may leave now, lieutenant. We'll meet this evening at the circus. I spoke to the head of the palace guard and he told me that you have been relieved from duty for the next two nights."

The circus tent was so immense that the Queen's palace and gardens could have fit inside it, with room to spare for trapeze artists to soar through the air, tightrope walkers to perch on their ropes high above, and Japanese gymnasts to circle around the arena, balancing on giant balls.

Nobody there, except for those who had seen the Hagia Sophia or the Duomo in Florence, had ever been inside such a colossal structure. The posters proclaimed that the circus had travelled the whole world, from New Zealand to America, and now it had come to Belgrade. It was rumoured that the real circus was in London at the time and the performance in Belgrade just a side show, but some found it inconceivable that anything could be more grandiose than what they were seeing. Everyone knew that Belgrade was anything but a lifeless, barren city of the East. The previous year, the famous traveller Sir Algernon Bunberry had published a travel guide in which he described his time in Belgrade ten years earlier, saying that any self-respecting gentleman would stay at least three nights in the city, enjoying its comforts. For the Serbs, the fact that the circus had stopped in Belgrade meant that their country was now firmly on the world map.

In Serbian lore, the Ottomans had for centuries held those lands by the nape of the neck, preventing them from becoming a country of their own. Treading on the world like a Japanese acrobat perched on top of a ball, the Ottomans had deluded themselves into believing that they ruled the globe. The truth of the matter, however, was that the world was turning and they were being left behind, less powerful than ever before.

Dragan was excitedly expounding on such patriotic themes in an attempt to pry Vesna's thoughts from the newspaper story, as they sat in one of the rows upon rows of wooden benches which ran around the circus ring. Gypsies were performing with their dancing bears and monkeys as people streamed into the tent, but their routine, which was seen on the streets every day and ill-suited to the grandeur of this setting, was a mere warm-up act for the real show.

But Vesna's thoughts were elsewhere. After a while, she turned to Dragan and smiled distractedly. Driven to paroxysms of enthusiasm by that glimmer of hope, Dragan launched into a harangue about the importance of travel guides, and the pride he felt because Belgrade was a favoured destination among European travellers. Soon enough, however, Vesna was rescued from his tirade by a boom that shook the very fabric of the tent.

The sound had come from a massive brass gong suspended by cables high above them. When a hush fell over the tent, a dwarfish red-haired announcer appeared. After greeting the audience first in French and then in German, he started to sing an aria in a resounding tenor. The audience looked at each other in confusion, and the children, who had been expecting clowns, were caught between surprise and fear. In the middle of the aria, the dwarfish announcer started doing backflips, singing all the while, and he continued flipping around the arena until the end of the song. As he held the very last note, he suddenly disappeared in a yellowish puff of smoke.

As the smoke in the tent dissipated, the audience saw that a man of gigantic proportions had appeared in the dwarf's place. He was wearing a leopard skin that left one shoulder bare, and a devilish leather mask adorned with ivory tusks. Five powerful-looking men appeared out of nowhere, rolling a stone with great difficulty towards the towering man. When he charged at them with a snarl, they scattered, and then he paused to look at the stone, polishing the tusks on his mask with a piece of canvas he held stretched between his hands. Suddenly he seemed to fly into a rage, spinning around on one leg several times—Dragan estimated at least fifteen—and emitting the most horrific of howls, until he finally came to a halt and brought his right hand down on the stone, splitting it in two. The audience gasped as one. Tugging at his leopard hide, the devil-man walked up to the split stone, picked up one of the halves with a grunt and heaved it into the air. The stone soared towards the middle of the arena and then disappeared into a hole in the ground that had suddenly appeared. After hurling the other half of the stone into the same hole, he wiped his hands on his thighs, ignoring the roar of applause.

At that moment there was another puff of smoke, from which appeared a woman holding a flaming hoop. She held it out at waist-level and a lion, its mane braided and adorned with pearls and gems, leapt through the flames, landing gracefully in front of the man in the mask before leaping back through the hoop. Next, the lion trainer held the flaming hoop up at head height and stamped her high-heeled boots three times, at which the lion leapt through the hoop again and roared, its mouth open wide, whereupon the masked man knelt down and placed his head in the lion's gaping jaws.

The lion closed its mouth gently but firmly around the man's neck, and began to growl. The audience held its breath. Then, very slowly, the man raised his right hand to the lion's throat and started choking it. The growling stopped and the lion began to writhe, its back paws scratching at the ground, but slowly the huge cat's muscles started to relax, until only its legs were twitching. As easily as if he were taking off a hat, the man removed his head from the lion's mouth and bellowed in triumph, at which point the lights in the tent suddenly went out.

The pearls braided into the lion's mane glimmered in a single beam of light. After a while the other lights slowly came back on, revealing the outlines of the caveman, the lion tamer and the lion, which was still lying motionless on the ground. As the lights went out again, the sounds of a piercing scream and growls echoed back and forth across the tent.

When his eyes had adjusted to the dark, Dragan noticed that Vesna was breathless, but he wasn't sure if it was out of fear or excitement. After a moment of hesitation he reached out and took her hand, which was clutching her knee. The fact that their hands had touched twice in the same day was more startling for him than the lion jumping through the burning hoop and nearly biting off a man's head.

In the darkness of the arena, a glowing form appeared, spinning round and round as furiously as if it were trying to drive right through the floor into the heart of the earth, tracing flames through the air. These twirling rings of fire flickered so quickly that, at first, no one in the tent could work out what they were.

But as the spinning slowed, it became clear that the form was a whirling dervish of sorts, arms rigid, one pointing up at the top of the tent and the other at the ground. Fire shot from his arms at regular points, balls of light burned along the hem of his skirt, and brief bursts of flame shot from the tips of his shoes with a whooshing sound.

As the dervish slowed, the audience's astonishment gave way to awe as they beheld the spectacle that was revealed before them. Dragan looked over at the flames reflected in Vesna's eyes, and he realized that he was still holding her hand. Blushing with the shame of having been so impertinent for a second time in a single day, the lieutenant pulled his hand away.

As the dervish sped up again, his skirt, which had begun to droop, billowed out again. The sound of drums filled the tent and the whooshing flames became a tornado of light once more. The sound of the taut leather drums drew the audience's heartbeat into its rhythm.

A sudden explosion rocked the tent and the flaming dervish rose into the air, only to plummet to the ground in a ball of fire.

Columns of fire shot from the man, who was now doubled over and writhing on the ground, shooting flames in all directions like a squadron of archers on a hilltop raining arrows down upon an enemy. It was only when Vesna saw the tent beginning to burn that she realized it wasn't part of the show.

The flames spread and engulfed the entire tent in flames. In the dark, no one could see the smoke billowing forth, but their eyes and noses were burning and they began trampling one another in the stands as they tried to rush out of the tent. When Dragan tried to take hold of Vesna's hand to lead her out, he was knocked down by the stampede.

Blinded by the darkness and choking on smoke, Dragan lost sight of Vesna. As people trampled over him, he felt his freshly healed ribs crack again. Knowing that he would choke to death if he didn't get out, he summoned the last of his strength and forced himself up. In the hope that it would ward off the swarming crowd he drew his sword, but in that chaos no one paid him any attention and he was shoved aside yet again. He swung out with the hilt of his sword to keep himself from falling to the ground, and knocked down a man who was stumbling along in front of him. Leaping over him, he cleared a path with the hilt and finally made it outside.

The right side of the tent was completely burnt and rags of flaming fabric floated down like a rain of phosphorescent insects.

As Dragan walked backwards gazing up at that majestic tower of flames, he heard someone calling his name. Turning in the direction of the voice, he saw Vesna, her face and clothes covered in soot.

Shaking him by the shoulders, she said, "Something's happening. I have to get back to the palace. You're in uniform, so stay here and help people as best you can." Then she ran off, dashing between people rolling around on the ground in a desperate attempt to put out the flames engulfing their clothes.

Dragan looked left and right. The field surrounding the tent was filled with people shouting, dashing around, and carrying the dead.

The circus was collapsing as it burned, but from a distance it looked like a ship sailing through the night, its sails filled with a red wind. Dragan was captivated by the spectacle, the likes of which he knew he'd probably never see again.

When he was young, Dragan had always enjoyed fairy tales, and his childhood was filled with them. He believed that there was a dragon lurking beneath every boulder and that there was an ill-starred princess waiting to be saved in every castle tower.

From fairy tales he knew that the immortal spirit of a monster lived on in the body of a bird that itself was sleeping in the heart of a fox high in the mountains. To overcome the undying beast you had to go up into the mountains, find the fox, cut the poor creature's heart in two, pull the bird out, and let the monster's soul drift up into the air.

So as a child he set off down a path that led from the village to the town to catch a cat, imagining that he would cut it open so that he could pull out its heart.

With two vicious swipes of its claws, the cat he'd found in a field dashed little Dragan's dream of having the bird living in its heart chirp a song in the palm of his hand.

Perhaps that tabby would have been proud, if it had known that Dragan had thought of it as a fox that carried a bird in its heart, in the heart of a snow-covered forest where the trees swayed in the clouds. More likely, however, the cat was glad to have been saved from little Dragan's preposterous plan.

"Cats are always like that," Dragan thought, and elaborated on the story:

"One day the fox was bragging to the cat, saying that its enemies can never get hold of it because it knows a thousand tricks and a thousand ways to escape. The cat's tail sank in humility as it murmured, 'I only know of one way to escape.' One day a hunting party came by and a dozen greyhounds set off in pursuit of the cat and the fox. The cat climbed up a tree and escaped. By the time the fox had decided which trick it was going to use to get away, the greyhounds had already sunk their teeth into its beautiful throat."

The large tent pole, which had been swaying for some time, broke with a resounding "crack", sending embers flying across the field. The people watching from a distance saw that ship driven by red winds crash into a rocky outcrop and vanish.

Dragan decided to be a cat with nine lives rather than a fox. Without a second's thought he started running towards what remained of the tent, jumping over the dead and dying as he ordered the stragglers to flee. As he swung left and right with the hilt of his sword, he headed for a small opening in the tent that hadn't yet caught fire. But when he leapt through the opening he tripped over a smouldering beam, smacking his forehead on the ground as he fell.

The pain kept him alert as he crawled onwards, clambering over dead bodies. He didn't see any survivors. Still, Dragan shouldered his way through that scene of death and destruction, giving what he assumed to be the dervish's remains a wide berth. At one point he stood up and looked around, hoping to spot a sign of life, but just then the floor, now weakened by the fire, gave way. The lieutenant plunged downwards.

Unsurprised by the fact that he had hit his head again, he pondered the captain's words, wondering if perhaps material truths could only be apprehended through experience. Indeed, after being pummelled by boards, concrete, earth and fists, his head had arrived at a material truth that was quite solid.

This time, however, the lieutenant hadn't hit his head against a board, concrete or earth, but bone.

The lion's mane, adorned with pearls and jewels, was still smouldering. Choking on the black smoke, the lion had writhed in agony as the flames tore into its body, strewing its organs on the ground like a bucket of freshly cut fish cast onto a boat's deck. When the lieutenant had plummeted down, he'd hit his forehead against the lion's side, cracking one of its ribs with a snap.

Once, while waiting in the area below the stage for its turn to perform during a show in Salzburg, another lion with a decorated mane—actually the mane was fake, as the real one had fallen out in tufts after the lion was neutered—had decided to stave off its hunger pangs by devouring a rather talented make-up artist. After this gruesome event, the make-up artist's twin brother, a trapeze artist, went down in history as the first person to go on strike at a circus.

On another occasion, at a nameless village near Lake Constance, a strongman had hurled a boulder down into the space beneath the stage, breaking the arm of one of the gypsies' monkeys. Irritated no end by the monkey's screeching a Japanese tightrope walker killed the monkey, and then one of the gypsies, with a barrage of throwing stars, but since the members of the circus lived on the fringes of society the matter was never taken to court.

And when the circus was in Deauville, on the shores of the English Channel, the cook, who had a penchant for pleasuring himself on fresh lamb livers, had scratched his arm on a nail brown with rust, while he was under the stage getting supplies. Within two months, tetanus led to lockjaw and the cook shuffled off his culinary coil.

Doubtless these are just a few of the many misadventures that had taken place in this shrine that was home to so many secrets.

As Dragan staggered to his feet, he realized with a sinking heart that his sword had broken in the fall and the blade was now lost among the lion's organs scattered on the floor. It was a ceremonial sword, good for little other than looking impressive on parade, but still Dragan cursed its loss. Despite his setback, he was determined to hew a heroic future for himself. Taking a deep breath, he thrust what was left of his sword into the scabbard hanging at his waist.

Just then, Dragan spotted what appeared to be a machine encircled by serpentine glass tubes inside of which filaments glowed dully in the darkness. Some of the tubes were lying in pieces, shattered by the beam that had crashed down under Dragan's weight, but he could hear the cogs of a whirring gearbox rattling against one another somewhere inside the machine.

He examined the apparatus in the dim light, knowing that reconnaissance is the key to all military matters. If you don't know the lay of the land, there's little chance of success in battle or executing a smooth retreat, which explained why Dragan had paid the price for his blind rush into the tent with a broken sword and two welts on his forehead.

Reaching out to brace himself, he took hold of a steel lever on the machine. The steel was hot—not yet hot enough to burn his hand, but getting hotter by the second.

As he proceeded farther along, his eyes now accustomed to the dark, he found that his path was blocked by a boulder, and then the machine's slowing clatter was replaced by a massive rumble as the entire floor of that ill-fated stage collapsed, bringing the raging orgy of flaming timbers thundering down like an army breaking through a battlefront. Everything disappeared under the burning debris: the lion, the mysterious machine, the magicians' props, the piles of pulleys and ropes...

Dragan found himself doubled over, pinned under the weight of a beam, his right cheek pressed against the boulder as cinders seared the back of his neck. As he felt the cinders burning deeper into his flesh, he regretted the fact that he would not die a beautiful death. He recalled a poem befitting his sense of regret:

"Everyone is defeated in war / Tsars and sultans alike fall under the blade / A young soldier, his right hand and left foot hewn off in battle / His once proud chest now crushed / Drifts into the glowing waters of a lake / And a haloed angel lifts him up / Washing his wounds in the cool clear water / And ruby wine and ambrosia / Ah, haloed angel, outwit the Devil."

As he muttered the last lines, preparing to make his final salute in this world, he felt the weight on his back lighten as the beam was pushed away.

A man wearing a leopard skin picked Dragan up and carried him over his bare shoulder down a short tunnel. Dragan sighed, "Ah, angel, haloed angel" and surrendered to his saviour.

"Lieutenant, I specifically requested the leopard skin. Most circus strongmen prefer jaguar skins because they have large spots, but the spots on a leopard skin, while smaller, are closer together and more orderly. People like to wear big, showy patterns because they want to seem impressive, not because they are. Let me emphasize that point—it's because of how they want to be seen. First you desire something and then you take on the form of that which you desire. If you want to shape someone according to your will, you have to know what they truly want. You can't shape someone into something they don't desire. If a jaguar doesn't want small spots, it's not going to happen."

He finished with a brief cough, which turned into a small coughing fit. When he had caught his breath, he went on: "Of course, that only holds true given the nature of the material at hand. For example, the circus tent didn't burn because it wanted to. No, it burned because it didn't object to burning. In other words, it didn't want to catch fire but at the same time it couldn't resist burning. So in the end it accepted the possibility that it might catch fire. Did it want to? No. Did it object? No. That's how the worst comes about, for both people and things."

As Dragan came round, he realized that he was sitting in a small room propped up against a wall. He had hoped to wake to the sight of an angel, but to his chagrin he found himself face to face with the strongman from the circus. Still wearing his mask, the strongman was rambling on about matters that struck Dragan as being not only irrelevant but also quite irksome.

"In any case, lieutenant, digressing is only useful if you're playing a game of three-card Monte. One person is distracted and the other person wins their money. Balance and harmony! If someone loses their money but no one else wins it, the balance is upset. And if you upset the balance, harmony is lost. If harmony is lost, it doesn't mean anything if a jaguar wants to have big showy spots. When that meaning is lost, it becomes preposterous for me to prefer wearing a leopard skin rather than a jaguar skin because my existence would cease to matter."

He leant in so close that the polished leather of his mask pressed against Dragan's nose.

"Alfred de Musset. He was a master of digression. But in the end he has a way of getting to the story. What was it that he said? 'How glorious it is—and also so painful—to be an exception.' That's a nice quote, isn't it?"

As the masked man's words echoed in his ears, Dragan's eyes widened in confusion. Just a few moments earlier he'd been waiting for death, his cheek pressed against a boulder, and now he was being subjected to a barrage of inanities of the most irrelevant sort.

Dragan may not have objected to dying with the stamp of a searing hot boulder on his cheek, because he had done it in the name of heroism and commitment. He did, however, have enough pride to object to the ramblings of a half-naked wild man wearing a mask. First, he didn't know the first thing about exotic animals, and second, he couldn't give a damn about the difference between jaguars' and leopards' pelts. In his view, it was pointless to talk about any animal that didn't live in the mountains, rivers and forests of Serbia. Watching them for the pleasure of a spectacle was one thing, but talking about them while in the throes of death was quite another. Dragan was of the opinion that expecting a modicum of seriousness during difficult times was a matter of human dignity.

While he had no objection to drawing on other cultures if it was done in the service of his people and country, to his mind the wild animals of some uncivilized jungle country could do nothing to serve his lofty ideals. If a symbol of speed or strength was needed, just turn to the wolf, he thought, which abounded in Serbia. True, wolves may not have spots, but in the depths of winter, is there really any need to go around dressed as garishly as a clown? In the end, he concluded that only lazy, decadent nations would look favourably on such colourful furs.

A wave of fury rushed through Dragan. He was determined to dash that daemon's nefarious plans, even if it meant that his ruby-red blood would seep into the soil of his nation.

The lieutenant braced himself with his hands and then, as nimble as the circus acrobats who had now met their maker, he leapt to his feet with a wolf-like howl. The masked man reared back, after having instinctively punched Dragan in the stomach.

Young Dragan, whose fit of patriotic love had consumed his last reserves of strength, exhaled once from his soot-filled lungs and, believing that this time he was truly going to die, passed out.

But he wasn't destined to enjoy the bliss of unconsciousness for long. He woke up and found himself in the exact same position he'd been in before. Not only that, he was also still facing the same mask.

The man wearing the leopard skin stood up and took off his mask, revealing a soot-covered face. He picked up a pitcher, poured a small amount of water into his hand and started to wash himself. The soot had worked its way deep into his pores, but as the strongman scrubbed himself Celal's features slowly emerged. At ease in his leopard hide as if it were his daily attire, Celal then threw the water that remained in the pitcher in Dragan's face.

Dragan sprang to his feet and saluted as the water ran down his face, only noticing that his right boot was missing when he attempted to stamp his heel.

"Dragan Petrovic, some rather unexpected things have happened today. *Primo*, hoping that I would find some survivors I went back into the tent one last time and found you curled up next to a rock. The unexpected thing was that I came upon that scene, not the scene itself. You see, there's nothing unexpected about coming across you in the most unlikely place in the midst of chaos and confusion. *Secundo*, as if it wasn't enough that the dervish blew himself up, the tent burned down and, according to my initial calculations, more than three hundred people died in the blaze along with one lion and three monkeys. *Tertio*, our fake dervish wasn't the type to commit suicide—believe me, he wasn't—but he was an incredibly irritating man, always grinding his teeth. Until this day I've never seen anyone who irritated me commit suicide. It seems that someone placed some explosives in his fire-resistant underpants. That was very unexpected."

Still saluting, Dragan said, "Captain!", but Celal silenced him with a wave of his hand and walked over to a large open-mouthed sack that was sitting in the corner. After rummaging through the sack for a few moments, he pulled out a military uniform and started putting it on.

"As you'll recall, I was telling you that leopard hides have small, orderly spots. When you find yourself dealing with an unexpected situation, you have to connect the dots. That's the only way to see the big picture."

Celal carefully placed the hide on the floor as if laying it out in front of a fireplace.

"Let's not be unfair, lieutenant. Some people see the large dots first. But coming upon the truth so quickly can be too disturbing. When you see what's really going on, life seems to go on for ever. The worst part about it is that life no longer seems worth living, because the mystery is gone. From one large truth a thousand smaller truths emerge, truths that wise people transform into poetry and bequeath to the world. Prophets and the great philosophers are people like that."

Celal glanced at Dragan and then started digging through the sack again, tossing things out left and right.

"Seeing as we're not prophets or great philosophers, we don't see the big picture. In any case, you can't make someone become something they don't want to be. We're not prophets or philosophers precisely because that's not what we desire. Anyone can become one or the other if that's what they truly want, even if it means becoming a second-rate prophet or philosopher. But we're not like that, are we Dragan? We're going to set off with the small, orderly spots of the leopard, not the showy ones of the jaguar. This, young lieutenant, is what we call rationality."

He found a pair of boots at the bottom of the sack and handed them to Dragan.

"And at the moment, the small spots are telling me that the palace is going to be raided tonight."

Silently Dragan took the boots and put them on.

"There can't be any other explanation for the burning down of the tent. The spots also say that the fire changed certain things. My dear Dragan Petrovic, we must go to the palace at once, but we won't know which side to take until we get there. The universe is a balance of opposing forces and our very existence is throwing it off balance, so we have to set it right again. How will we do that? The universe will tell us how. As two survivors of the fire, we are now bound to each other by a contract signed in flames. I hope that my faith in you will not be misplaced."

12

The Mummified Lion

"' A LITTLE LION. Ah, a little lion. / It jumped through the hoops. / Up it jumped through flaming hoops. A little lion. Ah, a little lion. / Come, curl up beside me. My clown, what a jester is he / Always pulling off tricks / My clown, what a jester is he / Wait little one, wait your turn.'

"My governess taught me that ditty. I'd completely forgotten about it until today. I think I remembered it when I saw that the lion had burnt to death. 'A little lion…' May he rest in peace—although he wasn't actually little at all. I don't think he was as lucky as Jumbo the Elephant, who definitely wasn't little. Six tons!… Perhaps Jumbo wasn't really so lucky either, but his owners were, in a way. Jumbo got hit by a freight train after a performance and died on the spot. Even if you weigh six tons, a train is a train, after all. They had bought Jumbo from the Zoological Society of London for ten thousand dollars, and within a year he'd brought in six hundred thousand. But he was worth more dead than alive. When he died they had him mummified, and even more people came to see the mummified elephant. As if that weren't enough they ground his beautiful teeth into a powder and mixed it with jelly. The richest people in New York lined up and spent a fortune to get a taste of it.

"I wonder if people would come to see the lion if we got it mummified. I've been thinking about that, but I don't imagine they would. For one thing, it's half-burnt. And we never even named the lion. It was always, 'Lion do this, lion do that.' But what were we supposed to do? It's a bit chilly in here. Can you find me a blanket or something?"

Céline was talking non-stop as she walked into the room, her words echoing off the walls like machine-gun fire. With each sudden movement she made, ash came sprinkling down from her hair. Embarrassed by his broken sword, Dragan had slunk off into a corner of the room.

Celal walked over to the sack and rooted through it, but when he couldn't find anything he took off his hooded cape and draped it over her shoulders, closing the collar with a silver chain.

Spreading out the dark blue cape, Céline laughed and said, "Thank you, Celal. Now, if everyone's ready, let's go. The carriage is waiting for us. We don't want it to turn it into a pumpkin now, do we? After all, we're going to a palace to attend a ball—of sorts." She slipped the hood over her head and motioned for Celal and Dragan to follow her.

With Céline in the lead, they walked out of the door. In the distance the tent was still burning. A brightly painted circus caravan approached, the driver holding the reins of two white horses whose bridles were adorned with massive red feathers, like the plumes of Roman legionaries. They clambered into the carriage and set off for the palace.

Dragan leant towards Celal and whispered, "Captain, why is this woman calling you Celal? And why are you working in a circus? Is Vesna okay? What's going on here?"

The caravan jolted as it rolled over a large rock in the road, sending Dragan careening towards Céline. When Dragan opened his eyes again, he found that he was lying with his head in her lap. Céline stopped twirling her curls and looked down at him with her blue eyes. Flustered, Dragan scrambled into the far corner.

Céline slid open a window at the front of the caravan and called to the driver: "Are we going to make it in time? Hey there, I said are we going to get there in time? Monsieur, can you hear me? Are we late?"

In the dim light, the driver's face was barely discernible, little more than a thick, rather sloppily waxed moustache that hung over his upper lip, and a chin that hadn't been shaved for days. The moustache twitched as he said, "Circus company… A determinant construction. 'Circus' comes from the Greek word for ring. Circus performances take place in a ring, so that part's easy. 'Company' is a little more complicated. Comes from the Latin, meaning 'to break bread together'. We might make it in time. But then again, we might not. It's difficult to give a definitive answer when conditions can change so suddenly. Especially with this caravan and these horses. So who knows, we might break bread together. Or not."

The driver's voice was drowned out at times by the rattling of the wagon, the sound of the wind and the neighing of the horses.

Celal recognized the man's voice. "Ah, Mr Commissioner. Your jurisdiction appears to be quite large indeed."

"Even bigger than you think, Celal. Seeing as you're a writer of sorts, I would've thought you'd make shrewder observations. True, aside from the occasional description of—what shall we call them?—'bayonets' in your novels, you don't delve much into military matters. But here you are, wearing the military uniform of a captain in the Serbian army. My commissioner title is just one of my epithets. You see, Celal Bey, we spies have our own unique sense of humour. Sometimes our work of smoke and mirrors suits the titles we use. So there is no need for you to call me 'Mr Commissioner'. 'Commissioner' will do just fine. But if you'll allow me, I should concentrate on driving to make sure that I don't roll this caravan over."

The three passengers sat in silence. Dragan disliked foreign uniforms, and he disliked the fact that everyone was now calling the man he knew as Captain Jovanovic 'Celal', a name which sounded ominously Turkish to him. To make matters worse, they were all speaking French and the moustached driver had just confessed that he was a spy.

Céline shouted through the window, "Commissioner, stop. Commissioner! Stop! This guy certainly knows how to orate, but he would do well to learn how to listen... Commissioner, stop! Please stop!"

The caravan suddenly slowed and came to a halt.

Céline climbed down, followed by Dragan, who tossed his broken sword into some bushes by the side of the road.

They uncoupled the horses from the caravan. Céline and the Commissioner got on one horse and Celal and Dragan got on the other. As Dragan clung to Celal, he shouted, "Captain, why do they call you 'Celal'?"

Clutching the reins, Celal tersely replied, "It's my stage name."

"Why were you at the circus?"

"I was dismissed from the army, as you know. I needed a job."

"Why are we going to the palace?"

"I don't know. We'll find out when we get there. Vesna is there, isn't she?"

Vesna indeed was at the palace, as were King Alexander and Queen Draga. Radovan, the pastry chef, was there, along with the guards, some servants, the aide-de-camp and his assistant, a number of young clerks, a few of the gardeners and a handful of stuffy generals. They were all there. But there was no electricity.

The country may have been poor, but it wasn't so impoverished that the palace was bereft of electricity. Ever since the wiring had been installed, it had for the most part worked without fail.

A few months earlier the electricity in the ballroom, one of the first few rooms in the palace wired for electricity, had cut off during a reception at which the King and Queen had been expected. Gossip soon spread that a coup had been planned for that night, thwarted only at the last minute when the King and Queen decided not to attend. King Alexander had shrugged off the rumours, but it was then that Queen Draga ordered that her brother be crowned if anything were to happen to them.

Celal was able to make out the palace gates in the moonlight. Guards were holding up lanterns with trembling hands as they peered left and right into the night. The palace's electricity supply had been cut off after the King and Queen returned from a banquet and retired to their chambers. Concerned, the Commander of the Guards and Alexander's aide-de-camp had set out to request reinforcements, but to no avail—all the soldiers were busy trying to quell the chaos that had erupted in the city after the circus fire. Now he had set out lamps in the palace gardens, and ordered some of his men to patrol the street in front of the palace to prevent any assassins from sneaking inside. Ten soldiers emerged from the open gates holding lamps, their weak flames sputtering in the wind.

The soldiers started to fan out into the street, but they hadn't got far when two white horses emerged from the night and bolted through their midst. Celal leapt to the ground and was immediately surrounded by guards, but he lashed out with such a flurry of blows that within seconds they were all lying at his feet. In the meantime, Céline rushed into the palace gardens, putting out the weakly glowing lamps placed here and there by smashing them with kicks and punches.

The Commissioner fired four shots into the air and then, despite the darkness, managed to shoot one of the soldiers in the shoulder as he stood frozen in fear. The Commander of the Guards rushed out of the palace when he heard the shots, only to catch a bullet in the side. The Commissioner dropped from his horse, raced over and pressed the barrel of his gun to the Commander's temple.

Just then, a bullet fired from a distance whizzed towards them, striking the Commander in the middle of the forehead. The Commissioner fired off a hail of bullets in reply, and soon the street was filled with the sound of gunfire, barked orders and groans of agony. Bodies thudded to the ground one after another, before a loud whinny cut through the tumult, followed by an even louder thud. After a moment of stunned silence, the palace lights came back on.

One of the horses was lying on its side, a trail of red running through its white coat. A pair of muddy boots was firmly planted in a pool of blood beside the horse.

Standing in the boots was Apis.

Dragan was still cowering in his saddle, his arms wrapped around the horse's neck. As with many things, the meaning of darkness was quite clear to Dragan: darkness was dark, and he couldn't see in the dark. So he reasoned that no one should expect him to fight in the dark. Now that the lights were burning again, he leapt down from the saddle.

It turned out that Apis, who now stood wiping his boots on the coat of the dead horse, had killed all the palace guards with his men and taken over the palace. He turned to Celal and said, "Glad to see that you weren't killed in the confusion."

"I was wondering if I could join the party. It would have been rather impolite for me not to show."

"Didn't you get our *singed* invitation?" Apis said with a dry laugh.

"Oh, that's very good," replied Celal.

Turning to two of his men, Apis snapped, "Watch them!"

The men trained their guns on Celal, Dragan and Céline.

The Commissioner approached Apis and said, "I thought they might cause us some trouble outside, so I brought them here. I thought that way we could keep an eye on them."

"Well done. I'll decide later what to do with them."

The large wooden door of the palace squeaked, giving away a soldier who was trying to close it. After firing a single shot that hit the soldier squarely between the eyes, Apis trotted into the palace with his men. Before following Apis inside, the Commissioner turned to Celal and said, "I know this isn't very gentlemanly of me. But Celal Bey, I just wish you'd listened to me when I warned you. Perhaps after all this is over we'll sit down and talk."

"Perhaps," Celal replied. "Perhaps we will."

13

Timelessness

D RAGAN PETROVIC did not spend that summer lost in dreams of marriage, because everything he believed in had been destroyed by a single stroke. Plunged into despair, the young lieutenant decided to purge from his very being all that remained of his previous life.

His desire to live was strong enough to prevent him from committing suicide. And since he wouldn't commit suicide, the only option for Dragan was to not be Dragan to the greatest possible extent.

That proved to be a struggle, because not being yourself first requires knowing yourself.

He remembered that they had stood in the palace garden in a state of timeless transience, like newly planted seedlings being buffeted by a storm. Dragan also recalled how that strange man called Jovanovic, or Celal, or whatever his name was, had wrenched the rifles from the men guarding them, bending the muzzles with his bare hands and knocking the soldiers to the ground. He also remembered falling flat on his face as he ran. As he struggled to erase his past self, the taste of that mouthful of gritty mud would surface from the depths of his memories time and time again.

He recalled that they had met up with Radovan, who he thought had been at the palace. Radovan had arranged a carriage for them, which Celal drove, and later they had switched carriages. He vaguely remembered walking through a forest for almost a week, and he could also recall that they had stolen some horses and ridden to a city he didn't recognize, before sneaking onto a train.

Eventually they arrived in Paris and made their way to a well-built two-storey house on the outskirts of the city. The first few days there were quiet. Celal hardly ever left his room and Céline was out all day, coming back only when dusk was approaching, with a basket of food.

They used the stove only to brew coffee, since none of them had much of an appetite, and they made do with salami, ham, cheese, bread and water.

That's when Dragan decided to vanquish his past self. First, he erased Vesna's face from his memory; he was so successful that he could no longer conjure up her image in his mind's eye.

He wondered if she'd been killed during the coup, or if she, like Radovan, hadn't been at the palace. As her visage disappeared from his memory, his own face started to vanish, too, whenever he looked in a mirror. Day by day Dragan became less himself.

Next he erased all thoughts of his own country, from the mountains, rivers and deepest of mole burrows to the eagles soaring in the heights—traces that he'd once felt were ingrained in his very being, and so he felt as if he were peeling a map of Serbia from his body.

As his face disappeared in the mirror, his body started disappearing as well.

All that remained was his desire to live and a yearning for love. In that sturdy two-storey building on the outskirts of Paris, Dragan yet again fell in love—this time with himself. But since he had purged himself of himself, he had difficulty identifying the object of his love. Although he was enraptured with himself, his passion was unrequited, which only stoked the fires of his obsession.

Eventually he realized that the only way he could satisfy his obsession was to indulge and spoil his love. So one morning he decided to leave the house, driven as he was by a pressing desire to enjoy the finest foods, drink the most exquisite wines and make voracious love.

By the time the young lieutenant reached the neighbourhood's square and gazed out along the streets of Paris, he had already erased from his thoughts all traces of that two-storey house with its garden.

14

A Rather Trying Matter

KING AND QUEEN KILLED IN BELGRADE PALACE COUP

ROYAL COUPLE BURIED IN THE SAME GRAVE

Telegram from our local correspondent

LONDON, 13TH JULY 1903

King Alexander and Queen Draga, Serbia's ruling monarchs, have been killed. After a military unit besieged the palace and overpowered the guards, assassins blasted open the door of the royal couple's bedroom with a bomb.

The King refused to be deposed by force and he shouted "Traitors!" at the assassins. The King was shot to death as he attempted to flee, and the Queen was killed with a bayonet.

The Chancellor, Minister of the Interior and Minister of War were killed in their homes, and the Queen's brother and sisters are also reported to have been killed.

The revolutionaries have appointed a new chancellor and the Serbian army has proclaimed Prince Karageorgevic as the new king. The Prince, who is currently in Geneva, immediately issued a statement saying that he had no involvement in the killings. The King and Queen were buried in the same grave in the cemetery of St Mark's Church in Belgrade.

Celal tore the story out of the newspaper, wadded it into a ball, and squeezed it in his fist until his stony fingernails cut into the flesh of his palm, drawing blood. Then he began to rake the soles of his feet against the bed's footboard. He was running a fever, and every shudder from his body sent a new rush of nausea through his stomach, not strong enough to let him vomit to get some relief, nor so weak that he could get to his feet. He was stuck with an unbearable queasy feeling.

After wiping his bloodied palm on the pillow, he tried to sit up but fell back on his elbows. In the end he managed to reach for a cool sachet of lavender on the bedside table, which he pressed against the cut in his palm. Getting to his knees on the bed, he supported himself on the wall with one hand and pressed the sachet of lavender to his nose with the other, taking deep breaths. The fever was making his head spin. Tearing open the sachet, he watched as the lavender spilt onto the pillow. By leaning down he managed to start licking up the dried seed pods. Although they only had a faint smell, they were so bitter that they burned his mouth and throat. He squeezed his eyes shut and tried to swallow some of the seeds, but a cough rising up from deep in his lungs made him double over again, and he vomited onto the pillow, against which his forehead was now pressed. This was followed by another round of vomiting, and then another. Feeling a little better, he pushed the pillow away and pulled the bed sheet aside. He pressed his face to the cool mattress, curled up and promptly fell asleep.

His head was lying between two pools of vomit, like the bust of a prince carefully placed on the bed. Flies were buzzing around the bust and the pools, and he awoke when they launched a vicious attack on his nose. He took a few moments to look around and assess his situation. Silently he got out of bed, opened the window, and pulled the bed sheets onto the floor.

He dragged the sheets downstairs and left them in front of the door to the garden. After a breath of fresh morning air, he went out to the back garden, where he collapsed beside a water pump behind a wooden screen. He filled a bucket of cool water from the pump and poured it over his head. He then removed his clothes and washed them, shivering in the cool morning air.

With a towel wrapped around his waist, he went into the kitchen to make himself a cup of coffee and roll a cigarette with some tobacco he found on a shelf. Céline walked in and said, "Admit it, you enjoy going around half-naked."

"Madame, I haven't been around much at all."

"Feeling groggy?"

"So groggy that I just want to go back to sleep."

"Looks like you need a shave, too."

"Well, I thought I should cover up my chin at least—it wouldn't do to be too half-naked."

Céline took a few sips of Celal's coffee and started pacing back and forth, holding the cup between her hands.

"Celal, go and get dressed. Our guest is going to be here soon."

She emptied the cup into the sink.

"By the way, you make a horrible cup of coffee."

Celal lit his cigarette.

"If you want me to look presentable, our guest must be a trying person. *Primo*, this is your house, so whoever's coming is your guest. *Secundo*, I myself am a guest of sorts here. Guests visiting guests… That's not the usual way of doing things. *Tertio*, that's how I like my coffee."

"Fine, go on and drink your tar, then. The word 'guest' is just a figure of speech. Jean has finally made it to Paris. He's staying at the Le Meurice on the rue de Rivoli. Did you know that it was the first hotel in Paris to have a telephone? It looks out over the Tuileries Garden. I love that place. We should go for a visit sometime. Anyway, he called while you were washing in the garden. He'll be here soon. I think."

"What do you mean, 'I think'?"

"The telephone is a great invention, but we could barely understand each other because of all the crackling. That's as much as I understood."

"Fine."

"Celal, melancholy doesn't suit you."

"Why not?"

"Just think of Aristotle."

Celal said nothing.

With a chuckle, Céline went on: "Aristotle believed that all geniuses—philosophers, scholars, poets and artists—suffer from melancholy. They're born with black bile. Take the case of Homer. If you'll recall the *Iliad*: 'But once he was stamped with the hatred of all the gods, he fled the sound of the footsteps of mankind, wandering alone with naught but his heavy heart.'"

"Meaning?"

"Accept it, Celal, you're not quite a genius. If you want to be able to suffer the pangs of melancholy, you have to be a genius. You're no hero from the *Iliad*, and the gods won't go out of their way to despise you. If someone's unworthy of melancholy, it just makes them dull and uninteresting."

"Céline, they killed everyone and we couldn't do anything about it. Maybe we even helped them in that massacre. What do you expect? Of course, let's forget about it. We'll just forget that they mutilated the King and Queen's corpses and threw them into a pile of manure in the garden. And Jean shouldn't go to the trouble of coming all the way here. Let's go to his fancy hotel with a telephone and have a feast. I promise not to be dull and uninteresting. And of course, we have to make sure that Madame is always in the highest of spirits."

"You don't say. What a wonderful idea. I wonder what truths are lurking in the ironic shallows of people suffering from melancholy. Very well then, I'll call Jean now. But my dear Celal Bey, please conduct yourself in a civilized manner. We're leaving in half an hour."

Celal offered a wan smile.

Céline said, "Look, Celal. No one ever became truly unhappy just because they couldn't understand the inner workings of another person's soul. But unhappiness is the only fate for those who are deaf to themselves."

They stopped in front of room 304 on the third floor of the Le Meurice. Céline rang the doorbell. Wearing his blond wig and fake moustache, Jean opened the door with an impish smile on his lips. After giving both of them a long hug, he bowed and invited them in.

They passed into the suite's sitting room. On the table was a tray of nearly two dozen oysters on ice. Jean picked up one of the oysters, sprinkled it with mignonette sauce and a squeeze of lemon, and sucked it down in two slurps. After popping a buttered piece of bread into his mouth and pouring champagne for everyone, he said, "We were nearly all killed because of that poor Swede."

Celal reached for an oyster. "Which Swede?"

"The whirling dervish who exploded. He's actually Swedish. He wasn't a bad painter, either. He found himself penniless in Paris. That's when I met him. I wouldn't be surprised if Paris was founded for the sole purpose of having artists go bankrupt. He was an anarchist at the time. Then again I was, too, before I started working for Sahir. I was a follower of Prince Kropotkin's. I was even tried in the Trial of the Thirty. Then I got tired of it all. When they started setting off bombs left and right, I decided to get out. That Swede was also put on trial, but unlike me he went to prison. When they let him out, he became interested in Islam and became a dervish. He even stayed in Cairo for a while. If you ask me, he was neither a dervish nor an anarchist, just a megalomaniac who couldn't squeeze his art onto a canvas, so in his own way he tried to turn his life into a work of art."

"Was the fire a coincidence?"

"It's hard to say these days how much of anything is a coincidence. I really don't know, Celal. I breathed in so much smoke that I ended up in hospital for two weeks. Apis could have finished off my work right there. No one knew anything about our plan to turn on the peace machine. It was probably destroyed in the fire, when the stage caved in. But one thing is certain. Apis took advantage of the fire and went ahead with his coup."

"And the Commissioner?"

"He works for an arms dealer. His work was done when a new king who would buy his guns came to power."

"So did the Swede decide to commit suicide?"

"It would appear that way. Apparently he met a Swiss dervish in Cairo, and they started publishing a magazine. Turns out the Swiss dervish was also an anarchist, who was in touch with certain Serbs involved in the movement. In those days, everyone in Switzerland was either a banker or an anarchist. But we all know that our Swede was also an explosives expert. Perhaps he decided to blow himself up on stage as a way to deliver a message to all the sovereigns of the world, as his artistic grand finale."

Celal squeezed some lemon juice onto his second oyster.

"Who's ever heard of a dervish committing suicide and taking hundreds of other people to the other world with him in the process?"

"My dear Celal, the entire world was probably founded upon a big misunderstanding. I'm quite certain that the order of dervishes would never ask anyone to blow himself up. But they found something in the Swede's room. I wrote it down somewhere. Just a moment, let me find it."

Jean went into the bedroom and came back with a piece of paper.

"Ah yes, here it is. It's probably a quote from Rumi: 'Someone who has learnt to ignite and illuminate the light in his heart cannot be burnt even by the sun. If you wish to shine like day, burn up the night of self-existence.' Celal,

I think that once a person decides to do something, they can find signs everywhere that point the way to what they want to do."

Céline cut in: "So the peace machine might still work, right?" She bit into a piece of buttered bread on which she'd placed some small pickles.

"There's no evidence that proves that it doesn't work. I still have my uncle Pierre's drawings and formulas. I can get everything needed to build it, in no time at all. Of course, what happened in Belgrade was terrible and we can't change that, but we can change what happens next. Céline, wasn't that young lieutenant with you all as well? You said he was close to the machine while it was still running. Where is he now?"

"I don't know. He came with us to Paris, but one morning he left and we haven't seen him since."

"It bodes ill," Celal said. "In difficult times, Lieutenant Dragan has an odd knack for getting himself into trouble."

With a smile, Jean said, "I think that all of us here share that knack."

Céline ate three oysters, one after the other, with no mignonette sauce or lemon juice.

"When can we activate the machine?"

"Well, mademoiselle, I may not have graduated but I was a student at the École Polytechnique. In no time at all."

*

199

Celal troubled himself little with the machine's technical details, as he realized that he would never grasp how it actually functioned.

He was confident, however, that Pierre's plans would work. A version of the peace machine had run, if only for a moment, in Belgrade. However, even if that amateur Swedish dervish hadn't committed suicide—just to burn up the night of his self-existence and to shine like the sun—and thrown the circus into bloody chaos, the effects of the machine would have been limited to a mere few kilometres. Belgrade simply didn't have the electrical power to allow the effects of the machine to spread very far.

All great writers may agree that, while there are ways to oppose military invasions, there is no force in the world which can resist the power of ideas. Therefore, it is impossible to create an object that is more powerful than an idea born at the right time.

And the time for the peace machine had come at last. The Paris Métro had opened only three years earlier, and the world's largest hydroelectric plant had been built just outside the city to power it. Pierre had calculated that in order to have the desired effect the machine would need to be powered by a massive amount of electricity, produced by rows upon rows of rumbling turbines. In Pierre's time no such plant had existed, but now the power that drove Paris's underground carriages was simply waiting to be hooked up to the peace machine.

As Celal, Jean and Céline approached the power plant in a horse-drawn rubbish cart, they knew that they were about to see turbines creating an electromagnetic field the likes of which the world had never seen before. The plant sat on the banks of the Seine, whose muddy waters sloshed noisily against the shore. The building gave off a whirring sound, as if it were about to burrow into the earth. Cautiously, the trio made their way along the back of the long building, until they came to a low door set in the wall. While the rest of the building appeared to be as heavily fortified as a castle, the door swung open as soon as they turned the handle. Jean knew that the power plant's guard was unfaithful to his wife once a month, at a particularly unsavoury bordello in Place de Clichy, so to convince the philanderer to leave the door open had been a matter of little difficulty.

Silently they unloaded the cart in front of the door. Jean examined a map of the plant by the light of a gas lamp, and guided them along its corridors to their destination. In a few trips they managed to carry all the parts of the peace machine to the main turbine hall.

Jean said, "The most important part is in the third sack. The envelope that arrived on Céline's birthday included the key to a storeroom, where we discovered the best samples Pierre had gathered from magnetic mountains all around the world. Thankfully, there are enough left to replace those we lost in Belgrade."

"When I was rescuing Dragan from the circus, I saw some long glass tubes that were broken."

"They were surrounding the magnetic stones in the heart of the machine. The electricity passing through them started a vibration in the magnets. But their effect was weak, and I doubt that they would have been strong enough to handle the current produced here. We need a lot of power, but not so much that we burn out the machine. Those tubes wouldn't have worked. We'll be using vacuum tubes no larger than your finger. They're in the first sack over there."

Jean worked for an hour setting up the machine, occasionally asking for Céline and Celal's help.

When it was finished, the machine was unlike anything they had seen before. Arcs of electricity flashed between forty-eight vacuum tubes, above which hovered a row of magnetic stones of various sizes connected to the tubes by cables, and the whole apparatus was enclosed in a glass bell. As electricity flowed through them, the tubes started to glow a faint red.

"The tubes are warming up. In about half an hour the peace machine will start emitting the first vibrations. We're lucky. They decided to redo the roof last week and took off all the copper sheeting, which means that the waves will radiate all the better."

Jean paused and looked around.

"Actually, we're not going about this the right way at all. We're about to change the course of world history, but none of us thought to bring a bottle of champagne! I refuse to allow the history books to record that peace was finally brought to the world by a bunch of bores who didn't know how to celebrate it properly."

"But, my dear Jean, you should know that I would never agree to go down in history like that." Reaching into a bag slung over her shoulder, Céline pulled out a bottle and started slowly undoing the wire over the cork. She paused.

Handing the bottle to Celal, she said, "Of course, I wouldn't want to sabotage world peace with an ill-aimed champagne cork. Would you care to do the honours without causing any damage to the machinery?"

"We've survived an exploding Swedish dervish and a burning circus tent collapsing around our ears—I don't think we need to worry too much about an errant champagne cork."

He took the champagne bottle from her hands, finished unwinding the wire, pointed it towards the door through which they had come, and popped the cork. After gurgling up a few spurts of white foam, the bottle seemed to relax.

"I do believe," Jean said with a smile, "that you forgot to bring glasses."

Laughing, Céline took the bottle and raised it to her lips.

At that moment they all froze as they heard the sound of approaching footsteps.

Jean placed himself between the machine and the door, arms spread wide.

Celal took a step back.

The footsteps were heading straight for the turbine hall.

Before they could see who was speaking, they heard a man's voice: "Unfortunately, I forgot to bring glasses, too… When children are playing and there is a sudden silence, it means that something is amiss. The length of the silence is commensurate with the extent of the trouble. I must admit, the circus really was not a good idea. So, there you are, my dear Celal Bey, and Jean, you're here, too. All this time I worked so hard for that damn circus, all for nothing. If I'd put you all in the ring as a clown act, I would've made more money."

It was Sahir. He held out his hands, palms up. "Don't worry. I'm alone and I'm unarmed."

He motioned towards the bottle of champagne. "After travelling all this way at this time of night, don't I deserve a sip, too?"

Taking the bottle from Céline, Celal handed it to Sahir. With a sigh, Sahir rested his chin on the mouth of the bottle and looked at Jean. "That wig isn't really your style, and that floppy moustache of yours does nothing to hide your identity. Did you really think that your life was in danger, just because you took Pierre's letter and worked out how to build the peace machine? Don't you think that if perchance it was possible, I would've done it myself? You thought that I didn't know about the plans in the letter, or the drawings. I was with Pierre before he went on his last trip and wrote that letter. I was the one who put it in an envelope and took it to the notary. Céline, at the very least he wanted to make sure that you knew what he had dedicated his life to, just in case anything happened to me. And Jean, you were always a foolish child but this time your foolishness is almost genius."

Jean adjusted his wig.

"Sahir, you sell guns. Of course you'd be opposed to the peace machine."

"I've known you since you were a child, Jean. If only you'd stopped to listen, none of this would have been necessary. There is no peace machine and there never will be. I tried for years to make one. But that's beside the point. Pierre spent years testing the machine on me."

The vacuum tubes were growing a deeper shade of red and started humming. After leaning down to tighten a few of them, Jean said, "It didn't work because we didn't have enough electricity. Sahir, you don't understand. The calculations are all there. It's our last chance of salvation before we destroy ourselves. You've seen the Zeppelin. How long will it be until they start bombing cities? Sahir, the solution lies in the problem. You know that. Pierre wrote it in his letter, and Arif said it too: 'The cure for every woe is hidden in the problem itself.' The cure for this new world run by engines and electricity is that very same technology. If we don't do something, we'll destroy each other. The peace machine was designed so that machines won't kill us all."

Sahir took a sip from the bottle. "Jean, this machine isn't going to bring peace to the world. But we can have faith in

the human race and, if we can take control of the government, if every country in the world becomes a democracy,
we can stop the slaughter—people won't let their countries
to go to war, especially if every country is armed as much as
the next. The human mind is capable of striking a balance,
and arms are a part of that balance. This machine adds
nothing to the power of thought. And without the power
of thought, what is left of humanity?"

The vacuum tubes surrounding the machine and leading towards the centre of the power station started glowing
more brightly, like lava expelled from a volcano.

Celal asked, "Why did you bring me all this way out here?
I found out who Karachiyano is. I know the whole story."

Sahir shot a concerned glance at the glowing vacuum
tubes. "I left it up to you to come or not. Celal, people have
to believe that they have free will. They have to decide if
they want peace or not, just as you decided to come to Paris.
You could have decided to stay in Istanbul. After talking to
the Commissioner in Marseille, you could've decided to take
the first ship home, or gone elsewhere."

Turning towards Sahir, Céline asked, "Don't you remember the story of King Midas and the donkey ears? Those
recordings you made when you acquired your first Edison
phonograph… you put your mouth next to the phonograph's
horn and spoke your deepest secrets. You said that one day
you'd go to Kudretköy and get your revenge. The recordings
are in a locked drawer, and you were sure that no one would

understand them because they're in Turkish. But you're not the only Turk in Paris, Sahir. After my father's letter came, I searched your place. When I found the recordings, I had one of Jean's regulars translate them for me. Didn't you obsess over the fact that Arif hadn't adopted you, but took Celal into his heart? And didn't you then try to take revenge by killing my father's and Arif's dreams? That's why you deal in arms—to take your revenge on the idea of peace."

Tears welled up in Celal's eyes. He took Sahir by the shoulders.

"Couldn't you just accept that you were a bastard, like me?"

"Celal, you're not a bastard. You're a child of the mountains, just as I am. Pierre wasn't wrong about everything. There is something about those magnetic mountains. I'll admit that I became almost obsessed with you, Celal. I wanted to know more about you. But not because, as Céline said, I was jealous of the attention that Arif lavished on you. It was out of sheer curiosity. I found out who you are and where you're from. You may even remember. Celal, you were born in Visoko, in Bosnia-Herzegovina, on the slope of a mountain. Céline, where were you born?"

Céline glared at Sahir. "You know the answer to that, so why are you asking me?"

"You were born in a house your family inherited from Pierre's grandfather on a slope of the hills of the Loire Valley. The name of the village is Les Noës. The road that runs past the village leads to the Madeleine Pass. The villagers there don't complain of the cold or hunger, but of the fact that their axes stick to certain stones when they go out to gather wood. Arif and I are from Mount Sipylus. None of us are bastards. Our parents are the magnetic mountains. The same is true for you as well, Jean. Where were you born? Where did you live until your father lost his dairy farm in which he'd invested his very last penny? In Quebec. The name of the town is Chartierville. When you were a mere child, Pierre visited your mother in the hope that he could convince her to return, and that's when he discovered the magnetic hill. Go to Côte Magnétique. It's just three quarters of an hour away. Pierre was right. People who were born exposed to a similar electromagnetic field are drawn to each other. They don't say 'Birds of a feather flock together' for nothing. But you can't use electromagnetic waves to affect people's minds. It goes against nature and the laws of science."

Celal snarled, "But that's not what you were saying before."

"I wasn't the one who drew you to Paris. You came for Céline. Now listen to me, what you have done here goes against both science and nature. For the sake of argument, let's imagine that the peace machine works and that humanity never again goes to war. We would have lost the free will that nature gave us. We would be nothing but lost, wandering souls. The human mind—and the soul—aren't so simple that they can be changed just by electrically charging some magnets. When we were in Vienna, we had long discussions with a doctor who is carrying out rather novel experiments in psychiatry. He helped me to comprehend what my soul already knew. From now on, illnesses of the soul will be treated by 'talking cures'. And this new theory doesn't only apply to individual treatment—what if we could 'talk' to everyone through newspapers, novels, even moving pictures? It might take longer, but we could achieve peace through free will."

The last few words that Sahir spoke seemed to be swept into a circle by the humming magnets, which suddenly established their own order, spinning on their own axes as they whirled around each other. As the spinning grew faster, the hum became louder.

Sahir pleaded, "I'm telling you, don't do this. The peace machine won't work. It will not bring peace. Pierre was right. The machine can affect the human mind but it won't bring peace, it will do nothing but drive you mad. The machine affects people who were born on magnetic mountains more than anyone else. Why did Dragan suddenly vanish? I'm telling you, nothing is a coincidence. Dragan was born in one of the villages on Mount Radan. You were all brought together by this magnetism. When the machine was turned on in Belgrade, it drove Dragan insane. Listen to me, you're not going to bring peace to the world, you're just going to unleash madness on it."

The magnets spun ever more quickly. The lights on the ceiling flickered on and off, and during the moments of darkness, the light of the sparks flashing between the magnets illuminated their faces. Celal grabbed Sahir's arms, twisting them behind his back. Sahir struggled, panting for breath, but he was unable to break free of Celal's grip. The hum of the machine had become a roar, drowning out the sound of the turbines. They all turned to look at the machine. The massive brass pipe suddenly spewed forth a shower of sparks, then started undulating like water rushing down the bed of an eternal stream as the rings within rings gave themselves over to the electromagnetic waves.

Even though he was still firmly in Celal's grip, Sahir managed to kick the nearly full bottle of champagne with the toe of his shoe. The bottle sailed through the air, spraying arcs of champagne, and exploded when it hit the machine's glass case. Champagne ran down the glass towards the vacuum tubes, and then trickled along the floor until it had almost reached the point where the tubes were plugged in. Jean tossed his wig on the ground before the advancing champagne, and it soaked up the trickle.

In a vain attempt to break free, Sahir lunged forward.

The steel frame of the power plant was now undulating to the same rhythm as the brass pipe.

All at once the roar ceased, but the peace machine and the steel framework continued to tremble in silence. The floor and the ceiling slid towards one another.

Celal let Sahir go, but both of them were riveted to the spot. Everything in the building was expanding and contracting in waves, but in a final contraction the machine and the building were disappearing. Everything solid was fading away. The floor was solid under their feet but appeared to be flowing. As the walls closed in on each other, they buckled outwards and then just as suddenly straightened out.

Sahir closed his eyes.

"They're late," he said.

The truth of the matter was that the Commissioner had grown tired of Sahir's paranoid obsession with the peace machine. He had neither assembled the arms company's private army, nor pulled any strings with people in the Ministry to have the power plant shut down that night, as Sahir had asked him to do. No, he had been enjoying a quiet night at home. He had fallen asleep at his desk with a bottle of wine as he sat there preparing to write his first novel.

15

The Peace Machine

IN THE DEAD OF NIGHT, the power plant suddenly lit up, waking up the nearby residents. The starless, moonless sky was set aglow with a phosphorescent light. People rushed to gather outside. No one was afraid of the strange glow. They weren't afraid of anything. The whirring sound that filled the air took on a physical form.

The ground was a taut drum.

Brrrum,

brrrum,

brrrum.

With each resonant beat the ground gently shook.

The whirring gave way to a mechanical melody.

Ra tata tat

Ra tata tat

Ra tata tat…

As the ground trembled, the melody seemed to hang in the air like a cloud. With every shift in the melody, the sky danced, first broadening, stretching out into an arch, and then collapsing in on itself.

The muddy waters of the Seine suddenly ran clear. As the people started making their way towards the banks of the river, the purple flowers of lilac trees drifted down over them. Small whirlpools churned in the river, matching the rhythm of the music. Like a huge censer, the power plant was giving off puffs of smoke which snaked into people's noses, filling their lungs.

One by one they slipped into the river's waters, which started flowing towards the city. The water slowly began to spread out, carrying with it the now serene music, the reflections of the glowing sky, and the people floating on its surface.

Everyone let themselves slip into the water: swindling butchers, clever washerwomen, accountants dreaming of being actors, old men who thought about their childhood cats now long dead, lovers, people looking for lovers to betray, moral and immoral counts, inventors, prostitutes, mussel gatherers, the blind, cowards afraid of becoming murderers, serial killers, the lazy, muscled men, outcasts, students, cook's assistants, cooks, cannibals, flower sellers, government officials, Bolsheviks, princes and the kings they couldn't kill, inventors, singers, soldiers of all ranks, gentlemen, wine makers, priests, clerics, bearded men enamoured of monkeys, the illiterate, people with torn trousers, the faithful, freed slaves, the lovelorn, troublesome youths, free-verse word slingers, people who fear rain, the paranoid, opium addicts, the mute and people who never spoke, vagrants and people who have lived well.

All of the world's rivers and seas, the oceans and flowing waters, became one.

The first to notice was an Englishman dressed as an Afghan mullah trying to cross the Hindu Kush into Peshawar. And then a shepherd in the Andes, a hermit at Aynaroz monastery, a dervish in the mountains of Khorasan, a ranger in the Alps. And then, finally, everyone.

An eagle circling over Mount Sipylus screeched and snapped its beak.

When the vibrations of the peace machine struck the slopes of all the mountains that Pierre had and hadn't climbed, they responded with a greeting in kind and turned into slow-motion waterfalls momentarily suspended in the air. Lifting everyone around them onto their backs, they then spread across the meadows of the earth. The people floating on the rippling waters of the world's rivers, seas and oceans glided towards one another.

Night and day were plucked away as if from a branch, as the petals of the lilac tree rained down, covering all the water and people. The sky and the water's surface merged into a mellifluous pale purple.

All of the living, the dead living on in memory, and the spectral bodies of the forgotten—all the cities, plains, mountains, valleys, swamps and garrisons—were swallowed up by the water, and they started to breathe a deep sigh of relief as they listened to that melody.

Brrrum,

brrrum,

brrrum…

Their own hearts started to beat together with the heart of the world.

Ra tata tat

Ra tata tat

Ra tata tat…

With the world's curious bliss, their found their own peace.

There was no more wild wheat—it had all been tamed.

Unafraid, the people tamed all the long-toothed wolves that had once snapped their ribs. They ignored the reeds whistling in the wind, and they set herds of white sheep to pasture with their hollowed reed pipes.

Uncowed by bitter blizzards, in huts of ice they told each other fairy tales.

From glass made from sand they made funhouse mirrors and cackled.

When someone fell in love but wept heartbrokenly and alone in a distant field of crops, the story was inscribed on a clay tablet with a nail dug out of the side of a mountain. For the sake of oases they fell in love with deserts and wept at every sunset. They tried to understand the tribulations of elephants and wild roses.

They were cruel. They captured the fish living a thousand floors down in the sea and the birds soaring a thousand floors up in the sky and devoured them. With maces they smashed in the heads of people so viciously that their pain was felt for miles around.

They were good. If a baby was sliding towards the open mouth of a crocodile, they risked their own lives to save it.

They were naïve, rushing headlong towards massive armies, beating their chests and bellowing.

They were as beautiful as green-headed mallards and cruel enough to take money for the number of soldiers' cocks they severed on battlefields.

They were human and they didn't know why they were there.

They were human and they would go on destroying each other.

Because they didn't know why there were there, they despised one another.

Even if they measured the size of the world with compasses and angle rules, even if they created anthologies of the work of all the poets written in dead languages, even if glaciologists measured the age of ice stalactites, even if oceanographers plumbed the deepest oceans, even if uranium glowed, cogs and gears followed every order, and trees were pruned and trained to fit in the palm of one's hand, they would go on destroying each other.

Though they solved the how, they couldn't work out the why. And so they despised each other.

Brrrum,

brrrum,

brrrum…

And the last resort—

Ra tata tat

Ra tata tat

They longed to be mechanized…

All the flowing waters of the world conjoined. All of the mountains in the world had become water.

Water ahoy, water ahoy, water ahoy.

All the people floating on their backs on the water that covered the world—side by side, hand in hand—had become a raft. On a planet with no land, their linked bodies were an undulating, drifting continent. Beneath lilac petals they murmured along with the melody that echoed from the surface of the sea to the sky and from the sky to the surface of the sea.

Those that were going to die hadn't died. Those that were going to be born were born. The dead had returned to life.

All the people who had come into the world and all those who would come into the world in the future were undulating together on that world of water. People who had died hundreds of thousands of years earlier smiled as they stroked the faces of newborn babies with their smooth hands. Every day there were more and more of them. Everyone's childhood, youth, old age, death and rebirth came into being alongside them. That massive human raft spread until it covered the entirety of the ocean.

The surface of the ocean-world embraced the future on

the shore of humanity's past and present and all possibilities. As the ocean-world grew heavier and heavier, it could no longer turn.

The world's cogwheel broke.

The melody that echoed from the water to the sky and from the sky to the water fell silent.

The ocean-world started to fall.

The people were terrified.

And the more frightened they became, the faster the world fell.

The brrrum was over.

All the people who had ever breathed in the scent of the world were now falling with it as they floated, hand in hand. Together they screamed, the philosophers and scribes, gentlewomen, maharajas and captives, the inventors of fire and the splitters of atoms, the first to think of burying the dead and the looters who burned the Library of Alexandria, people who had never been cooks, virgins or travellers who died of scurvy, and hunters who went off in search of deer but never returned.

The sound of their screams shook the water and sky. The sound of their cries made them more afraid. The sound of their cries emboldened them. And they screamed even more. Their voices zigzagged between the sky and the water, traversing the world. The water began to boil. The lilac petals shrivelled into black granules and sank.

Human Race of Nothingness.

Lost Human Race.
Non-Existent Human Race.
Surrender Human Race.
Give up.

Just one time the sun rose in the west. The mountains, valleys, meadows, seas and rivers were just where they should be. Just one time everyone in the world awoke at once. When they opened their eyes, the earth began to spin and circle around the sun.

Sahir, Celal, Jean and Céline awoke on the floor of the power station. Slowly they sat up and Céline started whistling the melody she'd heard in her dream. As the others got to their feet, they began to whistle the same melody. Céline walked down the corridor and went out through the door, which was still open, and continued walking. One by one the people living near the power station stretched and yawned as they stirred themselves from sleep. They were all whistling the same melody.

As Céline walked, she passed by people looking at each other in amazement as they explained the dream they'd had. In every corner of the world, everyone was whistling the same melody at the same time, bewildered that they had all had the same dream. Céline walked on and on, whistling. Like a ghost she wandered streets, alleys and dead ends, until at last she found her way.

She arrived at the building in the rue de Vaugirard where Sahir lived. She opened the door to the flat with her key and went into Sahir's study. She wound up the phonograph on the mahogany table and, after meticulously cleaning the recording cylinder, she clicked it into place. When she was sure that it was recording, she leant in towards the horn and said, "My name is Céline and last night I had a dream."

BINOCULAR VISION

EDITH PEARLMAN

'A genius of the short story' Mark Lawson, *Guardian*

IN THE BEGINNING WAS THE SEA

TOMÁS GONZÁLEZ

'Smoothly intriguing narrative, with its touches of sinister,
Patricia Highsmith-like menace' *Irish Times*

BEWARE OF PITY

STEFAN ZWEIG

'Zweig's fictional masterpiece' *Guardian*

THE ENCOUNTER

PETRU POPESCU

'A book that suggests new ways of looking at the world
and our place within it' *Sunday Telegraph*

WAKE UP, SIR!

JONATHAN AMES

'The novel is extremely funny but it is also sad and
poignant, and almost incredibly clever' *Guardian*

THE WORLD OF YESTERDAY

STEFAN ZWEIG

'*The World of Yesterday* is one of the greatest memoirs of the twentieth
century, as perfect in its evocation of the world Zweig loved, as it is
in its portrayal of how that world was destroyed' David Hare

WAKING LIONS

AYELET GUNDAR-GOSHEN

'A literary thriller that is used as a vehicle to explore big
moral issues. I loved everything about it' *Daily Mail*

FOR A LITTLE WHILE

RICK BASS

'Bass is, hands down, a master of the short form, creating in a few pages
a natural world of mythic proportions' *New York Times Book Review*